序　言

　　很多同學問，如何才能學好英文文法呢？讀了那麼多文法書，爲什麼還不會？我認爲，**學好文法，最簡單的方法，就是做練習題，不會做的題目再查文法書**。這樣，題目愈做愈有興趣，考試時會寫，英文文法也通了。

　　一般文法練習題，都是從名詞、動詞開始分類，照這樣分類，會使讀者限於狹窄的範圍，容易猜到答案，做到後面，前面又忘記了，對文法沒有全面性的了解，最糟的是，很快就會失去興趣，放棄文法。

　　本書共有 50 回測驗題，每回測驗只有 10 題，讀者做了會很有成就感，每條題目都是一個挑戰，看自己進步了多少。本書每條題目，都是從國內外大規模考試中，整理出來的，文法題考來考去，其實都很類似。我們刻意將文法規則打散，均勻分佈在每回測驗中，如果做了哪一條題目不會，可以看詳解，也可查閱「**文法寶典**」。在本書最後，我們也將所有題目按文法類別歸納，方便讀者查閱。

　　英文要學好，一定要學會文法，文法是一種歸納，把公認爲最好的語言表達方法，歸納成規則，這樣子，我們說出來或寫出來，就不會有錯誤。但是，規則也有很多例外，往往例外的、特殊的，也就是常考的，只要讀通這本書，相信你的英文文法，就會有相當的程度。

編者　謹識

TEST 1

Directions: *Of the four choices given after each sentence, choose the one most suitable for filling in the blank.*

1. If I _____ the truth, I would tell you.
    (A) know
    (B) have known
    (C) knew
    (D) will know   (   )

2. This is _____ house for such a small family.
    (A) too big
    (B) too big a
    (C) too a big
    (D) big too a   (   )

3. Jack was caught _____ on the exam.
    (A) cheat
    (B) cheated
    (C) cheating
    (D) being cheated   (   )

4. Eric is _____ tennis player on his team.
    (A) the much best
    (B) very the best
    (C) much the better
    (D) by far the best   (   )

5. You cannot be _____ when choosing friends.
    (A) too careful
    (B) more careful
    (C) so much careful
    (D) too much careful   (   )

6. I would _____ see the movie. It's too violent.

   (A) not rather
   (B) rather not
   (C) rather not to
   (D) like not to   (   )

7. You shouldn't have bothered, Mrs. Owens; you're
   _____ to me.

   (A) much too kind
   (B) too much kind
   (C) very much kind
   (D) very too kind   (   )

8. Mary is a good cook, and _____ .

   (A) so I do
   (B) so do I
   (C) so I am
   (D) so am I   (   )

9. When she has a lot of homework, she burns the midnight
   oil more often than _____.

   (A) not
   (B) none
   (C) ever
   (D) never   (   )

10. Two of these three students can speak English; _____
    cannot.

    (A) another
    (B) other
    (C) the other
    (D) the others   (   )

TEST 1 詳解

1. (**C**) If I **knew** the truth, I **would tell** you.
   如果我知道真相，我就會告訴你。

   表「與現在事實相反的假設」，其公式為：

   $$If + S. + \begin{cases} were \\ 過去式動詞 \\ 過去式助動詞 + V. \end{cases} \cdots, S. + \begin{cases} should \\ would \\ could \\ might \end{cases} + V.$$

2. (**B**) This is **too big a house** for such a small family.
   這間房子對這樣的小家庭來說太大了。

   so, as, too, how + 形容詞 + *a* + 名詞。（詳見文法寶典 p.216）

3. (**C**) Jack **was caught cheating** on the exam.
   傑克被發現考試作弊。

   catch sb. + *V-ing* 撞見某人正在
   被動語態是「*sb. is caught* + *V-ing*」，表「某人被撞見正在」。

4. (**D**) Eric is **by far the best** tennis player on his team.
   艾瑞克顯然是他那一隊最佳的網球選手。

   $$\begin{cases} the\ very \\ much\ the \\ by\ far\ the \\ far\ and\ away\ the \end{cases} + 最高級形容詞$$

5. (**A**) You **cannot** be **too** careful when choosing friends.
   選擇朋友時，再怎麼小心也不為過。

   cannot too 再怎麼～也不為過；愈～愈好

6. (**B**) I *would rather not* see the movie. It's *too* violent.

我寧可不看那部電影。太暴力了。

> *would rather* + *V.* 寧願
> $\begin{cases} \textit{would rather not} + \textit{V.} \text{ 寧願不} \\ = \textit{wouldn't rather} + \textit{V.} \text{ (不可寫成 } \textit{would not rather}) \end{cases}$
>
> violent (ˈvaɪələnt) *adj.* 暴力的

7. (**A**) You shouldn't have bothered, Mrs. Owens; you're *much too kind* to me.

歐文斯太太，妳實在不用麻煩的；妳對我真是太好了。

> 副詞 much 須放在 too 的前面，用來加強語氣。
> *much too kind* 太好了（不可說成 *too much kind*）

8. (**D**) Mary is a good cook, and *so am I*.

瑪麗菜做得很好，我也是。

> 這類的題目有一個答題的祕訣，將省略的字補上去，如果合理，即是答案。像答案 (D) so am I 是 *so am I a good cook* 的省略。而 (C) so do I，不可能是 *so do I a good cook*（誤）的省略。so 在意義上等於 also 時，須倒裝。

9. (**A**) *When she has a lot of homework*, she burns the midnight oil *more often than not*.

當家庭作業很多時，她經常會熬夜。

> $\begin{cases} \textit{more often than not} \text{ 常常（是 often 的加強語氣）} \\ = \textit{as often as not} \end{cases}$
> *burn the midnight oil* 熬夜（= *sit up* = *stay up*）

10. (**C**) Two *of these three students* can speak English; *the other* cannot. 這三個學生中，有兩個會說英文；另一個不會。

> 三個裏面，剩下來一個，用 the other。剩下來兩個以上，就用 the others。（詳見文法寶典 p.141）

TEST 2

Directions: *Of the four choices given after each sentence, choose the one most suitable for filling in the blank.*

1. Foreign tourists are often surprised at the _____ prices of things in Tokyo.
   - (A) big
   - (B) high
   - (C) much
   - (D) expensive   ( )

2. _____ the medicine, and your pain will go away.
   - (A) If you take
   - (B) Take
   - (C) Taken
   - (D) Taking   ( )

3. We will go camping this weekend _____ it rains or not.
   - (A) whether
   - (B) which
   - (C) unless
   - (D) though   ( )

4. These kinds of books are _____ little value.
   - (A) having
   - (B) of
   - (C) with
   - (D) without   ( )

5. Our company offers _____ workweek, competitive salary and attractive benefits.
   - (A) five-day
   - (B) five-days
   - (C) a five-day
   - (D) a five-days   ( )

6. _____ what I had ordered, I called the mail-order company.
   - (A) Received not
   - (B) Not received
   - (C) Not having received
   - (D) Not to receive   (   )

7. Bill's car is nicer than _____ of my brother.
   - (A) one
   - (B) that
   - (C) it
   - (D) which   (   )

8. He could not _____ from smiling, though with a slight sense of guilt.
   - (A) avoid
   - (B) help
   - (C) refrain
   - (D) quit   (   )

9. There are a _____ of dolphins.
   - (A) herd
   - (B) flock
   - (C) swarm
   - (D) school   (   )

10. The opera starts at seven. We _____ be late.
    - (A) needn't
    - (B) mustn't
    - (C) don't have to
    - (D) haven't got to   (   )

TEST 2 詳解

1. (**B**) Foreign tourists are often surprised at the ***high prices*** *of*
things in Tokyo. 外國觀光客常覺得東京物價之高，令人十分驚訝。
price（價格）的高低，該用 high 和 low 來形容。

2. (**B**) ***Take*** *the medicine,* ***and*** your pain will go away.
吃了藥，你的疼痛就會消失。

> 祈使句，and～ 如果…，就
> = If you…，～
>
> 「吃」藥要用 take，不可用 *eat*。

3. (**A**) We will go camping this weekend ***whether*** *it rains* ***or not***.
不論是否下雨，我們這個週末都會去露營。

> ***whether～or not***「無論是否」，引導副詞子句修飾 go，表讓步，
> or not 不可省略。whether～or not 引導名詞子句的時候，or not
> 可以省略。（詳見文法寶典 p.484）
> camp〔kæmp〕*v.* 露營

4. (**B**) These kinds *of books* are ***of*** *little* **value**.
這些種類的書，沒什麼價值。

> ***of*** + 抽象名詞 = 形容詞。如：*of value* = *valuable*；*of use* = *useful*。

5. (**C**) Our company offers ***a five-day*** workweek, competitive
salary and attractive benefits.
我們公司週休二日，薪水不錯，而且福利十分吸引人。

> workweek 為可數名詞，前面須加冠詞 a。而「數字–名詞」所形成的複
> 合形容詞中，名詞一律用單數，故選 (C) *a five-day* workweek「週休二
> 日」。其他類似用法如：*a seven-year-old* boy（七歲的小男孩）等。
> workweek〔'wɜk,wik〕*n.* 一星期的總工作時間
> competitive〔kəm'pɛtətɪv〕*adj.* 有競爭力的

6. (**C**) <u>**Not having received**</u> *what I had ordered*, I called the mail-order company.

由於沒收到我所訂購的東西，所以我打了電話給郵購公司。

mail-order〔'mel‚ɔrdə〕*adj.* 郵購的

本句是由 *Because I hadn't received what*…轉化而來。

> 副詞子句改爲分詞構句，有四個步驟：①去連接詞（Because）。②去相同主詞（I）。③動詞改爲現在分詞（hadn't received → having not received）。④否定詞要置於分詞之前（Not having received…）。

7. (**B**) Bill's car is nicer *than* ***that*** *of my brother.*

比爾的車比我哥哥的車好。

> 爲避免重覆前面提過的名詞，單數名詞可用 that 代替，複數名詞可用 those 代替。

8. (**C**) He could not <u>***refrain from***</u> smiling, *though with a slight sense of guilt.* 雖然有點罪惡感，但他還是忍不住微笑。

refrain from 表「克制自己不要」。其餘選項的都直接接動名詞。

$$\begin{cases} \textbf{\textit{cannot refrain from}} + V\text{-}ing \text{ 忍不住} \\ = cannot\ avoid + V\text{-}ing = cannot\ help + V\text{-}ing \\ = cannot\ quit + V\text{-}ing = cannot\ stop + V\text{-}ing \end{cases}$$

9. (**D**) There are ***a*** <u>***school***</u> ***of*** dolphins. 那裏有一群海豚。

school 作「（魚）群」解。　***a school of dolphins*** 一群海豚

其他單位的用法爲：(A) ***a herd of cattle***「一群牛」，(B) ***a flock of birds***「一群鳥」，(C) ***a swarm of bees***「一群蜜蜂」。
（表「群」的集合名詞用法，詳見文法寶典 p.54）

dolphin〔'dɑlfɪn〕*n.* 海豚

10. (**B**) The opera starts *at seven.* We ***mustn't*** be late.

歌劇七點開始。我們絕不能遲到。

表「絕對禁止；絕對不能」，用 ***mustn't***。

TEST 3

Directions: *Of the four choices given after each sentence, choose the one most suitable for filling in the blank.*

1. If you were really interested in what I'm saying, you _____ staring out of the window.
   - (A) will be
   - (B) will have been
   - (C) would have been
   - (D) wouldn't be   ( )

2. The question _____ at today's meeting is whether we should postpone the plan till next month.
   - (A) discussing
   - (B) is discussed
   - (C) to be discussed
   - (D) to be discussing   ( )

3. She's going to _____ her father into buying a new car.
   - (A) say
   - (B) speak
   - (C) talk
   - (D) tell   ( )

4. A violent demonstration must be avoided by _____ means.
   - (A) no
   - (B) all
   - (C) some
   - (D) none   ( )

5. Tom _____ breakfast at seven in the morning.
   - (A) is having always
   - (B) always is having
   - (C) has always
   - (D) always has   ( )

6. _____ will be the next president of the United States of America?

   (A) Do you think who
   (B) Who do you think
   (C) Who do you know
   (D) Whom do you think   (   )

7. Now that I have a motorcycle, I _____ ride my bicycle.

   (A) seldom never
   (B) ever seldom
   (C) hardly ever
   (D) hardly never   (   )

8. There is _____ when the patient will regain consciousness.

   (A) not to tell
   (B) no telling
   (C) not telling
   (D) only telling   (   )

9. He mentioned a book _____ I can't remember now.

   (A) which title
   (B) with the title which
   (C) in which the title
   (D) the title of which   (   )

10. The performance was so outstanding that the audience gave the musician a _____ ovation.

   (A) stand
   (B) stands
   (C) stood
   (D) standing   (   )

TEST 3 詳解

1. (**D**) *If you were really interested in what I'm saying*, you ***wouldn't be*** staring out of the window.

   如果你真的對我所說的感興趣,你就不會一直望著窗外。

   > 表「與現在事實相反的假設」,主要子句動詞用「should/would/ could/might + V.」,而用進行式有加強語氣的作用。
   >
   > stare〔stɛr〕*v.* 凝視

2. (**C**) The question ***to be discussed*** *at today's meeting* is *whether we should postpone the plan till next month*.

   今天會議所要討論的問題,就是我們是否要把這項計劃延到下個月。

   > 不定詞片語 to be discussed 做形容詞用,放在所修飾的名詞 question 之後,且依句意為被動,故選 (C)。 postpone〔post'pon〕*v.* 延期

3. (**C**) She's going to ***talk*** her father ***into*** buying a new car.

   她將去說服她的父親買部新車。

   > ***talk sb. into V-ing*** 說服某人

4. (**B**) A violent demonstration must be avoided ***by all means***.

   充滿暴力的示威運動一定要避免。

   > ***by all means*** 務必 (↔ *by no means* 絕不)
   >
   > demonstration〔͵dɛmən'streʃən〕*n.* 示威

5. (**D**) Tom ***always has*** breakfast *at seven in the morning*.

   湯姆總是在早上七點吃早餐。

   > **表現在的習慣動作,用現在簡單式。**
   >
   > ***always*** (總是) 為「頻率副詞」,其位置為:
   > ① be 動詞之後。② 一般動詞之前。③ 助動詞與一般動詞之間。
   > 本句中的 has (吃) 為一般動詞,故選 (D) ***always has***。

6. (**B**) Who ***do you think*** will be the next president of the United States of America? 你認為誰會是下一任美國總統？

> 凡是疑問詞所引導的名詞子句，做 think, believe, imagine, guess 等這類動詞的受詞時，必須把疑問詞放在句首。因為如不將疑問詞放句首，則該句無意義，如選項(A)。（詳見文法寶典 p.147）

7. (**C**) *Now that I have a motorcycle*, I ***hardly ever*** ride my bicycle.
既然我有了摩托車，我就很少騎腳踏車了。

> ***now that*** 既然　　***hardly ever*** 很少 (= *seldom*)

8. (**B**) ***There is no telling*** when the patient will regain consciousness.
沒有人知道病人何時會恢復意識。

> $\begin{cases} \textbf{\textit{There is no + V-ing}} & \cdots \text{是不可能的} \\ = \textit{It is impossible to + V.} \end{cases}$
>
> regain〔rɪ'gen〕*v.* 恢復　　consciousness〔'kɑnʃənsnɪs〕*n.* 意識

9. (**D**) He mentioned a book ***the title of which*** I *can't remember now*.
他提到一本書，但我現在無法記起它的書名。　　title〔'taɪtl〕*n.* 書名

> He mentioned a book ***the title of which*** I···
> = He mentioned a book ***whose title*** I···
>
> 關係代名詞 which 引導形容詞子句，修飾 book，在子句中，which 做 of 的受詞。

10. (**D**) The performance was *so* outstanding *that the audience gave the musician a **standing ovation***.
那場表演十分精彩，觀眾都起立為那位音樂家鼓掌歡呼。

> stand「站」為不及物動詞，沒有被動語態，故不能用過去分詞。
>
> ***standing ovation*** 起立鼓掌　　ovation〔o'veʃən〕*n.* 熱烈鼓掌、歡呼
> outstanding〔aʊt'stændɪŋ〕*adj.* 傑出的

TEST 4

Directions: *Of the four choices given after each sentence, choose the one most suitable for filling in the blank.*

1. You should prepare everything for tomorrow before you
   _____ to bed.

   (A) go
   (B) going
   (C) will go
   (D) are going   (   )

2. There was a drunken man _____ on his back in the street.

   (A) laid
   (B) lain
   (C) lying
   (D) laying   (   )

3. _____ do you think the population of San Francisco is?

   (A) How
   (B) How many
   (C) How large
   (D) How much   (   )

4. He didn't finish his homework, and _____.

   (A) either did I
   (B) so did I
   (C) I didn't, too
   (D) I didn't, either   (   )

5. Father gave me an expensive watch of Swiss _____ as my
   birthday present.

   (A) make
   (B) made
   (C) makes
   (D) making   (   )

6. The businessman was leading _____ to spend weekends with his family.

(A) a life so busy
(B) too busy a life
(C) so a busy life
(D) such busy a life   (   )

7. We haven't decided _____ to go to the movies or to go to the baseball game tonight.

(A) if
(B) which
(C) where
(D) whether   (   )

8. _____ in a very difficult situation, the doctor never had any rest.

(A) Work
(B) Working
(C) Worked
(D) To work   (   )

9. If I _____ about his illness, I would have visited him at the hospital.

(A) know
(B) have known
(C) had known
(D) might have known   (   )

10. They had a civil ceremony at the courthouse and the judge pronounced them _____ .

(A) husband and wife
(B) a husband and a wife
(C) the husband and the wife
(D) the husband and his wife   (   )

TEST 4 詳解

1. (**A**) You should prepare everything for tomorrow *before you go to bed.* 你應該在睡覺前,將明天要用的每樣東西準備好。

> 表時間或條件的副詞子句,須用現在式表未來,不可用 shall, will 表示未來。

2. (**C**) There was a drunken man *lying on his back in the street.* 街上有個醉漢平躺在地上。

> 本句是由…*a drunken man who lay on his back*…簡化而來。
>
> $\begin{cases} \textbf{\textit{lie}} & \textbf{\textit{lay}} & \textbf{\textit{lain}} & \textbf{\textit{lying}} & \text{躺} \\ \text{lay} & \text{laid} & \text{laid} & \text{laying} & \text{放置} \end{cases}$
>
> 背這個動詞變化有一個祕訣,把 lay laid laid laying 看成半規則 動詞,類似的有 pay paid paid paying。
>
> drunken〔'drʌŋkən〕*adj.* 喝醉的　　*lie on one's back* 平躺

3. (**C**) How *large* do you think the *population of San Francisco* is? 你認爲舊金山的人口有多少?

> population (人口) 的多或少,須用 large 或 small 來形容。

4. (**D**) He didn't finish his homework, and I didn't, *either.* 他沒寫完家庭作業,我也一樣。

> 肯定句的「也」,用 too;否定句的「也」,用 either 表示。
>
> $\begin{cases} \sim, \text{ and I did} \textbf{\textit{n't, either.}} \\ = \sim, \text{ and } \textbf{\textit{neither}} \text{ did I.} \end{cases}$

5. (**A**) Father gave me *an expensive watch of Swiss make* as my birthday present. 爸爸給我一隻昂貴的瑞士手錶,做爲我的生日禮物。

> make 可當名詞,表「品牌;~製」。
>
> *a watch of Swiss make* 瑞士製的手錶　　Swiss〔swɪs〕*adj.* 瑞士的

6. (**B**) The businessman was leading *too busy* a life *to spend* weekends with his family.

那位商人過著非常忙碌的生活，以致於無法和家人共度週末。

　　too…to 太…以致於不（不定詞表否定的結果）

　　{ lead *so* busy a life *that* 過著如此忙碌的生活，以致於
　　{ = lead *such* a busy life *that*

7. (**D**) We haven't decided *whether* to go to the movies *or* to go to the baseball game tonight.

我們尚未決定，今晚是要去看電影，還是去看棒球比賽。

　　whether…or 連接兩個不定詞，做 decide 的受詞。

8. (**B**) *Working* in a very difficult situation, the doctor never had any rest.

由於那位醫生處境艱困（也許人手不夠，病人太多等），他從來無法休息。

　　原句是由 *Because he was working in a*…轉化而來。
　　副詞子句改為分詞構句的步驟：①去連接詞（Because）。②去相同主詞（he，也就是 the doctor）。③動詞改為現在分詞（worked → working）。

9. (**C**) *If I had known* about his illness, I *would have visited* him at the hospital. 假如當時我知道他生病，我就會去醫院看他。

　　表「與過去事實相反的假設」，其公式為：
　　If + S. + *had* + p.p…, S + *should / would / could / might* + *have* + p.p.

10. (**A**) They had a civil ceremony *at the courthouse* and the judge pronounced them *husband and wife*.

他們在法院舉行公證結婚，法官宣佈他們結為夫妻。

　　civil ceremony 公證結婚　　courthouse〔'kort,haus〕*n.* 法院

　　┌──┐
　　│ 表示兩人之間的關係，不須加冠詞。如：*husband and wife*（夫妻）、│
　　│ *brother and sister*（兄妹）、*boyfriend and girlfriend*（男女朋友）。│
　　└──┘

TEST 5

Directions: *Of the four choices given after each sentence, choose the one most suitable for filling in the blank.*

1. All things _____, Mr. Smith is a very good husband.
   - (A) considered
   - (B) considering
   - (C) having considered
   - (D) to be considered ( )

2. Some are _____ his plan, while others are against it.
   - (A) as
   - (B) for
   - (C) with
   - (D) alike ( )

3. My younger brother has to serve in the military _____ beginning in September.
   - (A) two years ago
   - (B) for two years
   - (C) since two years
   - (D) during two years ( )

4. I'm sorry, but I forgot _____ the magazine you wanted.
   - (A) to buy
   - (B) buying
   - (C) of buying
   - (D) to have bought ( )

5. Who _____ has read Shakespeare's beautiful poems can forget their fascination?
   - (A) that
   - (B) which
   - (C) who
   - (D) whom ( )

6. This rose does not smell as sweet as _____ I bought the other day.

    (A) the one
    (B) it
    (C) such
    (D) which   (   )

7. One of my sisters is a lawyer; _____ are both doctors.

    (A) others
    (B) another ones
    (C) the others
    (D) some others   (   )

8. Jason regrets _____ harder when he was in college.

    (A) not to have studied
    (B) not having studied
    (C) having not studied
    (D) of having not studied   (   )

9. The mountains of Nepal are much higher than _____ of Japan.

    (A) those
    (B) this
    (C) these
    (D) that   (   )

10. Many TV talk shows are _____ programs.

    (A) life
    (B) live
    (C) alive
    (D) lived   (   )

TEST 5 詳解

1. (**A**) *All things considered*, Mr. Smith is a very good husband.
   如果把所有的事情都考慮在內，史密斯先生算是一個非常好的丈夫。

   > 本句是由 *If all things are considered, …*轉化而來。

2. (**B**) Some are *for* his plan, while others are *against* it.
   有些人贊成他的計劃，而有些人卻反對。

   > 介系詞 for 表「贊成」，against 表「反對」。 *for or against* 贊成或反對
   > *some…others* 有些…，有些

3. (**B**) My younger brother has to serve *in the military **for two**
   years* beginning in September. 我弟弟九月起，要服兵役兩年。

   > 表「持續（多久時間）」，介系詞用 *for*。
   > *serve in the military* 服兵役

4. (**A**) I'm sorry, but I *forgot to buy* the magazine *you wanted*.
   很抱歉，我忘了買你要的雜誌。

   > $\begin{cases} forget + to\ V. & 忘記去（動作未發生）\\ forget + V\text{-}ing & 忘記曾（動作已發生）\end{cases}$

5. (**A**) *Who **that** has read Shakespeare's beautiful poems* can
   forget their fascination?
   讀過莎士比亞優美的詩之後，誰能忘記它們的魅力？

   > 前面有疑問代名詞時，為了避免 "*Who who*" 或 "*Which which*" 的
   > 重複起見，關代須用 *that*。
   > Shakespeare ('∫ek,spɪr) *n.* 莎士比亞
   > fascination (,fæsṇ'e∫ən) *n.* 魅力

6. (**A**) This rose does not smell *as* sweet *as **the one** I bought the other day.*

這朵玫瑰不如我前幾天買的那朵香。

依句意，有指定是哪一個時，須加定冠詞。the one = the rose。

the other day 前幾天

7. (**C**) ***One** of my sisters* is a lawyer; ***the others*** are both doctors.

我有一個姐姐是律師；剩下的兩個姐姐是醫生。

在 one…the others 中，the others 是表示「其餘的；剩下的」。

8. (**B**) Jason regrets not having studied harder ***when** he was in college.* 傑森很後悔，大學時沒有更用功一點。

$\begin{cases} \textit{regret} + \textit{V-ing} & \text{後悔曾} \\ \textit{regret} + \textit{to V.} & \text{很遺憾要} \end{cases}$

否定字要放在動名詞前面，完成式的動名詞，表示比主要動詞先發生。

9. (**A**) The mountains *of Nepal* are *much* higher *than **those** of Japan.* 尼泊爾的山比日本的要高很多。

為避免重覆前面提過的名詞，單數名詞可用 that 代替，複數名詞則用 those 代替。those = the mountains。

Nepal〔nɪ'pɔl〕 *n.* 尼泊爾

10. (**B**) Many TV talk shows are ***live*** programs.

很多電視的脫口秀都是現場節目。

依句意，選 (B) ***live***〔laɪv〕 *adj.* 現場的。

而 (C) alive〔ə'laɪv〕 *adj.* 活著的，則不合句意。

talk show （電視上的）脫口秀

TEST 6

Directions: *Of the four choices given after each sentence, choose the one most suitable for filling in the blank.*

1. _____ luck would have it, I was at home when he called.
   - (A) As
   - (B) If
   - (C) When
   - (D) Unless　　　　　　　　　　　　　( )

2. There were beautiful willow trees on _____ side of the river.
   - (A) nor
   - (B) both
   - (C) any
   - (D) either　　　　　　　　　　　　　( )

3. We cannot _____ see the star with the naked eye.
   - (A) help
   - (B) necessarily
   - (C) hardly
   - (D) scarcely　　　　　　　　　　　　( )

4. I know little of mathematics, _____ of physics.
   - (A) still less
   - (B) much more
   - (C) rather more
   - (D) more or less　　　　　　　　　　( )

5. The juvenile delinquent denied _____ the motorcycle.
   - (A) to steal
   - (B) of stealing
   - (C) having stolen
   - (D) to have stolen　　　　　　　　　( )

6. Superstition has _____ that a black cat going across your path will bring you bad luck.

    (A) it
    (B) so
    (C) to
    (D) such   (   )

7. _____ with the wind and the rain, the game was spoiled.

    (A) How
    (B) What
    (C) Which
    (D) Why   (   )

8. We are going on a hike tomorrow, _____.

    (A) weather to permit
    (B) weather permitting
    (C) weather permits
    (D) for weather to permit   (   )

9. He did nothing _____ weep when he heard of his mother's death.

    (A) but
    (B) as
    (C) that
    (D) to   (   )

10. There are quite a _____ interesting things to see in this city.

    (A) many
    (B) number
    (C) few
    (D) much   (   )

TEST 6 詳解

1. (**A**) *As luck would have it*, I was at home *when he called.*
   他打電話來時，我幸好在家。

   > *as luck would have it* 幸運；不幸（視上下文而定）

2. (**D**) There were beautiful willow trees *on either side of the river.*
   河的兩岸有漂亮的柳樹。　　willow〔'wɪlo〕*n.* 柳樹

   > 河的兩岸可説成 *both sides* of the river，或 *either side* of the river。

3. (**B**) We can*not necessarily* see the star *with the naked eye.*
   我們用肉眼不一定看得見星星。

   > *not necessarily* 未必；不一定（= *not always*）（副詞的部份否定）
   > 而 (A) cannot help + V-ing「忍不住；不得不」，用法與句意均不合。
   > *the naked eye* 肉眼

4. (**A**) I know little of mathematics, *still less* of physics.
   我不太懂數學，物理學就更不用說了。

   > 表「更不用說」：
   >
   > | *much more*
= *still more*
= *even more* | （肯定句） | *much less*
= *still less*
= *even less* | （否定句） |
   > |---|---|---|---|
   >
   > little 為否定詞，故選 (A) *still less*。
   > 而 (D) more or less「或多或少」，則不合句意。

5. (**C**) The juvenile delinquent *denied having stolen* the motorcycle.
   那名少年犯否認偷了摩托車。

   > deny〔dɪ'naɪ〕*v.* 否認　　*deny* + V-ing 否認
   > having stolen 為動名詞的完成式，表比主要動作 denied 早發生。
   > juvenile〔'dʒuvə,naɪl〕*n.* 青少年　　delinquent〔dɪ'lɪŋkwənt〕*n.* 犯罪者

6. (**A**) ***Superstition has it that*** *a black cat going across your path will bring you bad luck.*

　　有種迷信的說法是，黑貓橫越你要走的路，會招致不幸。

　　　Superstition has it that 迷信指出

　　　其他類似的用法有：***Rumor has it that***「謠傳說」，***Legend has it that***「傳說指出」等。that 所引導的名詞子句，做 it 的同位語。

　　　superstition〔‚supɚˋstɪʃən〕*n.* 迷信　　path〔pæθ〕*n.* 去路

7. (**B**) *What with the wind and the rain*, the game was spoiled.

　　一方面因為起風，一方面也因為下雨，比賽就被破壞了。

　　　what with ~ and (what with) 一半因為～，一半因為
　　　what by ~ and (what by) 一半靠～，一半靠
　　　spoil〔spɔɪl〕*v.* 破壞

8. (**B**) We are going on a hike *tomorrow*, *weather permitting*.

　　天氣許可的話，我們明天就去健行。　　hike〔haɪk〕*n.* 健行

　　　原句是由…, *if weather permits.* 轉化而來。***weather permitting*** **常考，可以當慣用語一樣背下來。**

　　　（副詞子句改為分詞構句的步驟，詳見文法寶典 p.458）

9. (**A**) He ***did nothing but*** weep *when he heard of his mother's death.*

　　當他聽到母親的死訊，就只是哭。

　　　do nothing but + 原形 *V.* 只是　　weep〔wip〕*v.* 哭泣

10. (**C**) There are ***quite a few*** interesting things *to see in this city.*

　　在這個城市，可以看到很多有趣的事物。

quite a few	*quite a little*
= *not a few*	= *not a little*
= *a large number of*	= *a large amount of*
= *many* 很多（修飾可數名詞）	= *much* 很多（修飾不可數名詞）

TEST 7

Directions: *Of the four choices given after each sentence, choose the one most suitable for filling in the blank.*

1. I recognized him at once, as I had seen him _____.
   - (A) since
   - (B) before
   - (C) ago
   - (D) forward   (   )

2. The price of the house is now _____ it used to be.
   - (A) three times as high as
   - (B) as three times high as
   - (C) three times as expensive as
   - (D) as three times expensive as   (   )

3. _____ teaching French at college, Mr. Peterson teaches a class at a high school.
   - (A) His
   - (B) Beside
   - (C) Besides
   - (D) In addition   (   )

4. Certain medicines, _____, will turn out to be harmful.
   - (A) excessively used
   - (B) excessive using
   - (C) having excessively used
   - (D) having excessively been used   (   )

5. _____ records were imported from Germany.
   - (A) Almost
   - (B) Most of
   - (C) The most
   - (D) Almost all the   (   )

6. Five minutes earlier, _____ we could have caught the
   last train.

   (A) or
   (B) but
   (C) and
   (D) so   (   )

7. Linda is _____ more beautiful than Helen.

   (A) very
   (B) much
   (C) by far the
   (D) far and away the   (   )

8. Kate speaks English very fast. I've never heard English
   _____ so quickly.

   (A) speak
   (B) speaking
   (C) spoken
   (D) to speak   (   )

9. Two thirds of the work _____ finished.

   (A) are
   (B) did
   (C) is
   (D) will   (   )

10. A language may extend _____ national and cultural
    boundaries.

    (A) on
    (B) in
    (C) out
    (D) beyond   (   )

TEST 7 詳解

1. (**B**) I recognized him at once, *as I had seen him before*.
   我立刻就認出他，因為我以前看過他。

   > 「以前」見過他，用 before。而 ago 之前須有時間，如 two days ago
   > （兩天前）。 recognize〔ˈrɛkəgˌnaɪz〕*v.* 認出 *at once* 立刻

2. (**A**) The price *of the house* is now *three times as high as* it
   used to be. 那棟房子現在的價錢是以前的三倍。

   > price（價格）的高低，用 high 和 low 形容。東西的貴或便宜，才用
   > expensive 或 cheap 形容。

   > 倍數的表示法：$\begin{cases} ①倍數 + as + 形容詞 + as \\ ②倍數 + the + 名詞 + of \end{cases}$

3. (**C**) *Besides teaching French at college*, Mr. Peterson teaches
   a class at a high school.
   彼得生先生除了在大學教法文之外，還在高中教書。

   > $\begin{cases} besides \ 除了～之外（還有）\\ = in \ addition \ to \end{cases}$ $\begin{cases} beside \ 在～旁邊 \\ = next \ to \end{cases}$

4. (**A**) Certain medicines, *excessively used*, will turn out to be
   harmful. 有些藥如果使用過量，會是有害的。

   > 原句是由⋯, *if they are excessively used*, ⋯簡化而來。
   > excessively〔ɪkˈsɛsɪvlɪ〕*adv.* 過度地 *turn out* 結果（成為）

5. (**D**) *Almost all the* records were imported *from Germany*.
   幾乎所有的唱片，都是從德國進口的。

   > $\begin{cases} \text{All of } \textit{the} \text{ records} \\ \text{Some of } \textit{the} \text{ records} \\ \text{Most of } \textit{the} \text{ records} \end{cases}$ 都要有 *the*。

   > Almost all of the records 可簡化為 Almost all the records。
   > (A) Almost 為副詞，不可修飾名詞 records。(B) → Most of the records，
   > (C) → Most records (= *Most of the records*)。

6. (**C**) ***Five minutes earlier***, ***and*** we could have caught the last train.　要是早五分鐘，我們就能搭上最後一班火車。

> ｛ 祈使句，and～　如果…就
> ｛ = If + S. + V. ，～

> 祈使句中，如有「數詞 + 名詞」，則常省略動詞。本句等於 : *If we had been five minutes earlier*, we could have caught the last train.

7. (**B**) Linda is ***much*** more beautiful than Helen.
琳達比海倫漂亮多了。

> 修飾比較級形容詞，須用 ***much***。而 (A) very 修飾原級形容詞，(C) by far the 及 (D) far and away the 均用於修飾最高級形容詞。(參照 Test 1 第 4 題)

8. (**C**) Kate speaks English very fast. I've never ***heard English spoken*** so quickly.
凱特說英文說得很快。我從沒聽過英文能說得這麼快。

> hear 為感官動詞，其用法為：「hear + 受詞 + p.p.」表被動，英文是被說的，故選 (C) ***spoken***。

9. (**C**) Two thirds of ***the work is*** finished.
這項工作已完成三分之二了。　　two thirds　三分之二

> ｛ all / some
> ｛ most / the remainder
> ｛ half / the rest 　　　　　 ｝ + of + ｛ 單數 N. + V單
> ｛ part / 分數 (幾分之幾) 　 ｝ 　　　 ｛ 複數 N. + V複
> 　　　　　　　　　　　　　　　　　　 (詳見文法寶典 p.143)

10. (**D**) A language may extend ***beyond*** national and cultural boundaries.　語言能超越國家與文化的疆界。

> 介系詞 ***beyond*** 表「超過～的範圍」。
> extend〔ɪkˈstɛnd〕*v.* 延伸　　boundary〔ˈbaʊndərɪ〕*n.* 邊界；界限

TEST 8

Directions: *Of the four choices given after each sentence, choose the one most suitable for filling in the blank.*

1. She _____ be over thirty; she must still be in her twenties.
   - (A) may
   - (B) must
   - (C) oughtn't
   - (D) can't
            (　　)

2. _____ they will win the game in the end.
   - (A) No doubt
   - (B) Not doubt
   - (C) No doubtfully
   - (D) Not any doubt
            (　　)

3. Mr. White gave me _____ little money he had then.
   - (A) as
   - (B) that
   - (C) what
   - (D) which
            (　　)

4. I _____ stay poor than become rich by dishonest ways.
   - (A) would better
   - (B) would more
   - (C) would rather
   - (D) would like to
            (　　)

5. My stand _____ what it is, I have to oppose this idea.
   - (A) along
   - (B) being
   - (C) off
   - (D) on
            (　　)

6. Come what _____, she will not give up.

- (A) can
- (B) may
- (C) must
- (D) should   (   )

7. Work is not the object of life _____ than play is.

- (A) more
- (B) less
- (C) any more
- (D) anything more   (   )

8. We had a number of trees in our yard _____ down by the strong wind.

- (A) blow
- (B) blown
- (C) to blow
- (D) being blown   (   )

9. Students can't learn _____ facing some hardships.

- (A) but
- (B) whether
- (C) without
- (D) except for   (   )

10. It is common knowledge that cheese _____ milk.

- (A) makes
- (B) is made into
- (C) is made of
- (D) is made from   (   )

TEST 8 詳解

1.(**D**) She ***can't*** be over thirty; she must still be in her twenties.
   她不可能超過三十歲;她一定才二十幾歲。

   > 肯定的推測用 must,表「一定」;否定的推測用 ***can't***,表「不可能」。
   > ***be in one's twenties*** 某人二十幾歲的時候

2.(**A**) ***No doubt*** they will win the game in the end.
   無疑地,他們最後會贏得比賽。

   > $\begin{cases} \textbf{\textit{No doubt}} + \text{S.} + \text{V.} \quad \text{無疑地} \\ = \textit{There is no doubt that} + \text{S.} + \text{V.} \end{cases}$

3.(**C**) Mr. White gave me ***what little money he had*** then.
   懷特先生當時把他所僅有的一點錢都給了我。

   > ***what little money sb. has*** 某人所僅有的一點錢
   > **這條題目常考**,what 在此做關係形容詞,和關係代名詞一樣,可引導名詞子句。what 加上所修飾的字,用法和 what 一樣。
   > 而 ***what*** little money he had = ***all the*** little money ***that*** he had。
   > (詳見文法寶典 p.156、166)

4.(**C**) I ***would rather*** stay poor ***than*** become rich ***by dishonest ways***.
   我寧願窮,也不願靠不誠實的方法致富。

   > $\begin{cases} \textbf{\textit{would rather}} \sim \textbf{\textit{than}} \quad \text{寧願}\sim\text{也不願} \\ = \textit{had better} \sim \textit{than} \end{cases}$ stay〔ste〕*v.* 保持~的狀態

5.(**B**) ***My stand being what it is***, I have to oppose this idea.
   因為我的立場是如此,我必須反對這個想法。

   > 本句是由 *Because my stand is what it is,* I…轉化而來。
   > stand〔stænd〕*n.* 立場;想法　　oppose〔ə'poz〕*v.* 反對

6. (**B**) *Come what may*, she will not give up.

無論發生什麼事,她都不會放棄。

$\begin{cases} \textit{Come what may} \ 無論發生什麼事 \\ = \textit{Whatever may come} \end{cases}$

助動詞 may 表「可能」。(詳見文法寶典 p.360,530)

7. (**C**) Work is *not* the object of life *any more than* play is.

工作和遊樂都不是人生的目的。　　object〔'ɑbdʒɪkt〕*n.* 目標

$\begin{cases} \textit{not}\cdots\textit{any more than} \ 和\cdots一樣不 \\ = \textit{no more}\cdots\textit{than} \end{cases}$

8. (**B**) We *had* a number of trees *in our yard* *blown down* *by the strong wind.* 我們院子裏有幾棵樹被強風吹倒。

樹被強風吹倒,依句意爲被動,故用過去分詞 blown。

a number of ① 幾個(= *several*) ② 許多(= *many*)視前後句意決定意思。

9. (**C**) Students *can't* learn *without facing some hardships.*

學生要面對一些艱難困苦,才能從中學習。

「*not*…*without*」爲「雙重否定」的句型,表「每…必;無…不」。

face〔fes〕*v.* 面對　　hardship〔'hɑrd,ʃɪp〕*n.* 辛苦

10. (**D**) It is common knowledge *that cheese is made from milk.*

大家都知道,起司是由牛奶製成的。

$\begin{cases} \text{be made of} \ 由\sim製成(爲物理變化,看得出原料) \\ \textit{be made from} \ 由\sim製成(爲化學變化,看不出原料) \\ \text{be made into} \ 製成 \end{cases}$

(詳見文法寶典 p.575)

common knowledge 常識　　cheese〔tʃiz〕*n.* 起司

TEST 9

Directions: *Of the four choices given after each sentence, choose the one most suitable for filling in the blank.*

1. The man whose head had been shot was as _____ as dead.
   - (A) good
   - (B) well
   - (C) much
   - (D) ever   (　)

2. Let's walk a little faster _____ we should be late for school.
   - (A) fear
   - (B) unless
   - (C) lest
   - (D) so that   (　)

3. The day was rainy, and _____ was worse, it was stormy.
   - (A) so
   - (B) such
   - (C) what
   - (D) which   (　)

4. That is the restaurant _____ the Italian food was extremely good.
   - (A) that
   - (B) which
   - (C) at which
   - (D) on which   (　)

5. _____ that in August, 1984, my work obliged me to go to Japan.
   - (A) Happening was
   - (B) That happened
   - (C) I happened
   - (D) It happened   (　)

6. No sooner _____ begun his speech than he felt dizzy.

    (A) John has

    (B) has John

    (C) John had

    (D) had John   ( )

7. He is much happier now than _____.

    (A) ever before

    (B) never before

    (C) before ever

    (D) before never   ( )

8. _____ on the hill, the church commands a fine view.

    (A) Standing

    (B) Situating

    (C) Laying

    (D) Locating   ( )

9. Never in all my life _____ such a beautiful sunset.

    (A) saw I

    (B) I have seen

    (C) have I seen

    (D) I did see   ( )

10. He felt something cold _____ his right leg.

    (A) touched

    (B) to touch

    (C) touching

    (D) to have touched   ( )

TEST 9 詳解

1. (**A**) The man *whose head had been shot* was ***as good as*** dead.
那個頭部中槍的人，和死掉沒兩樣。

    as good as 和～一樣；幾乎 (= *almost*)   shoot〔ʃut〕*v.* 射擊

2. (**C**) Let's walk a little faster *lest we **should** be late for school.*
我們走快一點，以免上學遲到。

$$\left.\begin{matrix} that \\ so\ that \\ in\ order\ that \end{matrix}\right\} + S. + V. \qquad \left.\begin{matrix} lest \\ in\ case\ that \\ for\ fear\ that \end{matrix}\right\} + S. + (should) + V.$$

    以便於（表肯定目的）   以免（表否定目的）

3. (**C**) The day was rainy, and ***what was worse***, it was stormy.
天空正在下雨，更糟的是，似乎會有暴風雨。

    what is worse「更糟的是」，是常考的插入語。
    stormy〔'stɔrmɪ〕*adj.* 似乎有暴風雨的

4. (**C**) That is the restaurant ***at which*** the Italian food was

    extremely good. 那就是義大利菜做得很棒的那家餐廳。

    That is the restaurant ***at which*** the Italian…
    = That is the restaurant ***where*** the Italian…

5. (**D**) ***It happened that*** in August, 1984, my work obliged me to
go to Japan. 一九八四年八月，我碰巧因為工作，不得不去日本。

    It happens that 碰巧 (= *It chances that*)
    其他類似的用法還有：***It appears that***「似乎」、***It follows***
    that「由此推斷」等。
    oblige〔ə'blaɪdʒ〕*v.* 使不得不

6.(**D**) *No sooner **had John** begun his speech than he **felt** dizzy.*
約翰一開始演講，就覺得頭暈。　　dizzy〔ˋdɪzɪ〕*adj.* 頭暈的

> 「*No sooner* ＋ 過去完成式 ＋ *than* ＋ 過去式」，表「一…就」。
> no sooner…than 中的 no sooner 和過去完成式連用，本來過去完成式表示比過去式先發生的動作，但是 no sooner 中的 no 是副詞，等於 not at all，所以 no sooner…than 表「一點都不比…早發生」，因此和 than 之後的動詞，前後時間扯平。又 no sooner 是否定副詞，否定副詞放句首，助動詞須放在主詞前，形成倒裝。(詳見文法寶典 p.629)

7.(**A**) He is much happier now *than **ever before***.
他現在比以前快樂多了。

> ***than ever before*** 比以前　ever 用來加強 before 的語氣。

8.(**A**) ***Standing on the hill**, the church commands a fine view.*
那座教堂位於山丘上，俯瞰著美麗的風景。

> 本句是由 Because the church *stands* on the hill…轉化而來。
> 也可說成：Because the church *lies* on the hill…
> 　　　　 ＝ Because the church *is located* on the hill…
> 　　　　 ＝ Because the church *is situated* on the hill…
> 故 (B) 須改為 Situated，(C) 須改為 Lying，(D) 須改為 Located。
> command〔kəˋmænd〕*v.* 俯瞰　　view〔vju〕*n.* 風景

9.(**C**) ***Never in all my life** have I seen such a beautiful sunset.*
我這輩子從沒看過這麼漂亮的落日。

> 否定字 never 放句首，主詞與動詞須倒裝，其目的在使副詞片語接近所修飾的動詞片語 have seen。

10.(**C**) He *felt* something cold *touching* his right leg.
他覺得有個冰冷的東西碰到他的右腳。

> feel 為感官動詞，其用法為：feel ＋ 受詞 ＋ { V. (表主動)
> 　　　　　　　　　　　　　　　　　　 V-ing (表主動進行)
> 　　　　　　　　　　　　　　　　　　 p.p. (表被動)
> 依句意為主動，故空格應填 *touch* 或 *touching*，選 (C)。

TEST 10

Directions: *Of the four choices given after each sentence, choose the one most suitable for filling in the blank.*

1. _____ Mr. Smith, have you seen him lately?
   (A) Talking
   (B) Talking of
   (C) To talk
   (D) To talk about   (   )

2. I tried to take the dog out of our house, but he _____ go out.
   (A) were to
   (B) had to
   (C) might not
   (D) would not   (   )

3. _____ on the farm all day long, he was completely tired out.
   (A) Worked
   (B) Not working
   (C) Being working
   (D) Having worked   (   )

4. The baseball game had _____ started when it began to rain.
   (A) sooner
   (B) rarely
   (C) seldom
   (D) scarcely   (   )

5. You mustn't miss _____ this wonderful movie.
   (A) in seeing
   (B) seeing
   (C) to have seen
   (D) to see   (   )

6. Kevin loves to play golf among _____.

    (A) another thing

    (B) other things

    (C) other's things

    (D) the other things   ( )

7. It was so cold this afternoon that _____ anybody went swimming.

    (A) all

    (B) almost

    (C) hardly

    (D) most   ( )

8. I am no _____ able to operate this machine than he is.

    (A) far

    (B) much

    (C) very

    (D) more   ( )

9. My father is said to _____ really hard in his youth.

    (A) work

    (B) have worked

    (C) be working

    (D) be worked   ( )

10. We suffered from _____ troubles.

    (A) great many

    (B) greatly many

    (C) a great many

    (D) many a great   ( )

TEST 10 詳解

1. (**B**) *Talking of Mr. Smith*, have you seen him lately?
   說到史密斯先生，你最近見過他嗎？

   > ∫ *talking of* 談到　爲獨立分詞片語，置於句首，修飾全句。
   > ∫ = *speaking of*　（什麼是「獨立分詞片語」，詳見文法寶典 p.463）
   > lately ('letlɪ) *adv.* 最近

2. (**D**) I tried to take the dog out of our house, but he *would not* go out.
   我想帶那隻狗出門，但牠就是不肯出去。

   > 表「意志」，助動詞用 will，根據句意，要用過去式 would。

3. (**D**) *Having worked on the farm all day long*, he was completely tired out.
   在農場上工作了一整天，他真是累壞了。

   > 本句是由 *Because he had worked on the farm…* 轉化而來。
   > *be tired out* 筋疲力盡

4. (**D**) The baseball game had *scarcely* started *when it began to rain.*
   棒球比賽一開始，就下起雨了。

   > 表「一…就」的句型：
   >
   > S. + had + { *scarcely* / *hardly* } + p.p. + { *when* / *before* } + S. + 過去式 V.
   >
   > = S. + had + *no sooner* + p.p. + *than* + S. + 過去式 V.
   >
   > = *As soon as* + S. + 過去式 V. , S. + 過去式 V.

5. (**B**) You mustn't *miss seeing* this wonderful movie.
   你絕對不能錯過這部很棒的電影。

   > mustn't 表「絕對不能」。　*miss + V-ing* 錯過（miss 還可以表「想念」。）

6. (**B**) Kevin loves to play golf *among other things*.

凱文尤其喜歡打高爾夫球。　　golf〔gɑlf〕*n.* 高爾夫球

> *among other things* 尤其
> = *among others*

7. (**C**) It was *so* cold this afternoon *that hardly anybody went swimming*. 今天下午很冷，幾乎沒有人去游泳。

> 依句意，選 (C) *hardly*〔'hɑrdlɪ〕*adv.* 幾乎沒有。有些副詞可以修飾
> 名詞，像 not, only, also, even, hardly 等。(詳見文法寶典 p.228)
> *hardly anybody* 幾乎沒有人
> = *almost nobody*

8. (**D**) I am *no more* able to operate this machine *than he is*.
我和他一樣都不會操作這部機器。

> 做這類的題目，要背下面的例句：
> He is *no more* a god *than* we are. (他和我們一樣都不是神。)
> = He is *not* a god *any more than* we are.
> *no more…than* 和～一樣不
> = *not…any more than*

9. (**B**) My father is said to have worked *really hard in his youth*.
聽說我父親年輕時工作十分努力。

> 不定詞的完成式 to have worked 表比主要動作 is said 早發生。
> *be said to* 聽說　　*in one's youth* 在某人年輕的時候

10. (**C**) We suffered from *a great many* troubles.
我們遭受到很多的麻煩。

> *a great many* + 複數 N.　很多
> = *a good many* + 複數 N.　　　(詳見文法寶典 p.167)
> = *many a* + 單數 N.

TEST 11

Directions: *Of the four choices given after each sentence, choose the one most suitable for filling in the blank.*

1. Remember _____ I've just told you. It'll be very important when you grow up.

    (A) as
    (B) that
    (C) what
    (D) which   (   )

2. _____ by the sound of the door, I checked to see who it was.

    (A) Startle
    (B) Startled
    (C) To startle
    (D) Startling   (   )

3. The ten-year-old boy cannot so _____ as sign his name.

    (A) far
    (B) good
    (C) long
    (D) much   (   )

4. He stole, _____ to get things for himself as to get a thrill from it.

    (A) as well
    (B) not rather
    (C) not so much
    (D) for as much   (   )

5. Everything in the universe is _____ matter or energy.

    (A) either
    (B) neither
    (C) whether
    (D) whatever   (   )

6. Please include a self-addressed, stamped envelope if you would like the photos _____.

    (A) return
    (B) returned
    (C) returning
    (D) to return   (   )

7. Statistics _____ a required course for majors in economics.

    (A) are
    (B) is
    (C) are being
    (D) is being   (   )

8. If the sun _____ in the west, she would marry you.

    (A) rises
    (B) risen
    (C) was to rise
    (D) were to rise   (   )

9. She is always _____ the ball.

    (A) to miss
    (B) missed
    (C) missing
    (D) being missed   (   )

10. He is good at reading, but his listening ability is _____ average.

    (A) below
    (B) beyond
    (C) behind
    (D) within   (   )

TEST 11 詳解

1. (**C**) Remember *what I've just told you*. It'll be very important
   名　詞　子　句
   when you grow up.
   記住我剛剛對你說的話。當你長大以後，這將會是非常重要的。

   > what 引導名詞子句，做 remember 的受詞，在子句中，what 做 told
   > 的直接受詞，what = the thing that。

2. (**B**) *Startled by the sound of the door*, I checked to see *who it was*.
   由於被門的聲音嚇了一跳，所以我去看看到底是誰。

   > 本句是由 *Because I was startled by the sound*…轉化而來。
   > startle (ˈstɑrtl̩) v. 使驚嚇　　check (tʃɛk) v. 查看

3. (**D**) The ten-year-old boy *cannot so **much** as* sign his name.
   那位十歲的小男孩甚至連簽名都不會。

   > $\begin{cases} not\ so\ much\ as\ 連\sim 都不 \\ = not\ even \end{cases}$

   > 例：I have *not so much as* heard his name.
   > 　　（我連他名字都沒有聽說過。）（詳見文法寶典 p.536）

4. (**C**) He stole, ***not so much** to get things for himself **as to get***
   a thrill from it.
   他偷東西，與其說是拿東西給自己，倒不如說是想從中獲得刺激。

   > $\begin{cases} not\ so\ much\ A\ as\ B\ 與其說是 A，不如說是 B \\ = not\ A\ but\ B \end{cases}$

   > thrill (θrɪl) n. 興奮；刺激

5. (**A**) Everything *in the universe* is ***either*** matter *or* energy.
   宇宙中的一切，不是物質，就是能量。

   > ***either*** A ***or*** B 不是 A 就是 B　　universe (ˈjunəˌvɝs) n. 宇宙
   > matter (ˈmætɚ) n. 物質　　energy (ˈɛnɚdʒɪ) n. 能量

6. (**B**) Please include a self-addressed, stamped envelope *if you would like the photos **returned**.*

如果想退回照片的話，請附上有回郵地址的信封。

> *would like* + 受詞 + $\begin{cases} \text{V-ing（表主動）} \\ \text{p.p.（表被動）} \end{cases}$ 喜歡；想要
>
> *would like = want*
>
> self-addressed〔ˏsɛlfəˊdrɛst〕*adj.* 有寄信人姓名住址的
>
> stamped〔stæmpt〕*adj.* 貼上郵票的

7. (**B**) *Statistics is* a required course for majors in economics.

統計學對主修經濟學的學生而言，是必修的科目。

> statistics〔stəˊtɪstɪks〕*n.* 統計學
>
> *required course* 必修的科目   major〔ˊmedʒɚ〕*n.* 主修學生

> 學科、疾病的名稱，雖然形式為複數，但意義為單數，因此須接單數動詞。
> 如：statistics（統計學）、mathematics（數學）、physics（物理學）、
> 　　politics（政治學）、economics（經濟學）、linguistics（語言學）；
> 　　diabetes（糖尿病）、measles（麻疹）等。

8. (**D**) *If the sun **were to rise** in the west,* she *would marry* you.

如果太陽從西邊出來，她就會嫁給你。

> 在 If 子句中，「*were to* + *V.*」，表與未來事實相反的假設。

9. (**C**) She is always <u>missing</u> the ball.　她老是漏接球。

> 現在進行式與 always、constantly、all the time 等表「連續」的時
> 間副詞連用，表示說話者認為不良的習慣，或不耐煩之意。（詳見文法寶
> 典 P.342）　　miss〔mɪs〕*v.* 漏接

10. (**A**) He is good at reading, but his listening ability is *below average.*　他的閱讀能力強，但聽力就低於一般水準。

> 介系詞 *below* 表「在～之下」。
>
> *below average* 在平均水準以下　　*be good at* 精通

TEST 12

Directions: *Of the four choices given after each sentence, choose the one most suitable for filling in the blank.*

1. I have never seen such a good dancer. She is really _____.
   - (A) anybody
   - (B) anything
   - (C) something
   - (D) everyone   (   )

2. Health is above wealth, for _____ can't bring us so much happiness as _____.
   - (A) this, that
   - (B) that, this
   - (C) these, those
   - (D) those, these   (   )

3. _____ to it that such a thing does not happen again.
   - (A) Do
   - (B) Mind
   - (C) See
   - (D) Watch   (   )

4. The audience gave the singer a big hand. _____, he tried to express his thanks.
   - (A) Deeply moved
   - (B) Having been moving
   - (C) Having moved
   - (D) Moving   (   )

5. Jack seldom, _____, goes to church on Sundays.
   - (A) if any
   - (B) if ever
   - (C) if anything
   - (D) if necessary   (   )

6. Jeff and Jenny saved _____ they could to visit their uncle in Hawaii.

    (A) as a lot of money as
    (B) as much money as
    (C) money as a lot as
    (D) money as possible as   (   )

7. He had to carry _____ from his house to the station.

    (A) much luggage
    (B) so many luggages
    (C) three pieces of luggages
    (D) many luggage   (   )

8. What is it _____ you really want to say?

    (A) what
    (B) how
    (C) that
    (D) where   (   )

9. _____ seems easy at first often turns out to be difficult.

    (A) It
    (B) That
    (C) What
    (D) Which   (   )

10. I spent the last few days _____ those historic sites.

    (A) visit
    (B) visited
    (C) visiting
    (D) to visit   (   )

TEST 12 詳解

1. (**C**) I have never seen such a good dancer. *She is really <u>something</u>*.
   我從沒見過有人舞能跳得這麼好。她真是了不起。

   > something 可表「了不起的人或事」；nothing 則表示「沒什麼」。
   > 又如 somebody 指「大人物」，而 nobody 則是指「小人物」。

2. (**A**) Health is above wealth, *for <u>this</u> can't bring us so much happiness as <u>that</u>*.
   健康重於財富，因為財富帶給我們的快樂，不比健康多。

   > this 指較近的，that 指較遠的。

3. (**C**) *<u>See to it that</u> such a thing does not happen again.*
   注意，不要讓這種事再發生。

   > 「*See (to it) that* +子句」，字面的意思是「看著它做」，表示「務必；留意」。

4. (**A**) The audience gave the singer a big hand. *<u>Deeply moved</u>, he tried to express his thanks.*
   觀眾給予那位歌手熱烈的掌聲。歌手覺得非常感動，想要表達感謝之意。

   > 本句是由 *Because he was deeply moved,* he…轉化而來。
   > ***give sb. a big hand*** 給某人熱烈鼓掌
   > move〔muv〕*v.* 使感動

5. (**B**) Jack *<u>seldom, if ever</u>,* goes to church on Sundays.
   傑克就算曾經，也很少在星期天上教堂。

   > ***go to church*** 上教堂做禮拜

   > if ever 是副詞子句的插入語，只是省略了主詞和動詞而已，表「即使曾經，也很少」。其他常見的還有 if possible, if necessary, if any, if not 等。(詳見文法寶典 p.653)

6. (**B**) Jeff and Jenny saved *as* much money *as they could* to visit their uncle in Hawaii.

傑夫和珍妮爲了要去夏威夷拜訪叔叔，所以儘可能地存錢。

> ⎰ *as ~ as one can* 儘可能
> ⎱ = *as ~ as possible*
>
> save〔sev〕*v.* 存（錢）

7. (**A**) He had to carry *much luggage* *from his house to the station.*

他必須從家裏提很多行李去車站。

> luggage〔'lʌgɪdʒ〕*n.* 行李，看來似普通名詞，卻是不可數名詞，所以用 much 修飾。但如果是指一件一件行李，要用單位名詞 piece 表示。三件行李，就可說成 *three pieces of luggage*。
>
> carry〔'kærɪ〕*v.* 攜帶；搬運

8. (**C**) What is it *that* you really want to say?

你到底想說什麼？

> 強調句型：「It is + 強調部份 + that + 其餘部份」，因爲強調部份是疑問代名詞 what，而 what 又必須置於句首，故變成 What is it that…?。(詳見文法寶典 p.115)

9. (**C**) *What* seems easy at first often turns out to be difficult.

起初似乎很容易的事，結果往往會變得很困難。

> 複合關代 what 引導名詞子句，做主詞，what = the thing which。
>
> *turn out* 結果（成爲）

10. (**C**) I *spent* the last few days *visiting those historic sites.*

我利用最後幾天的時間，去遊覽那些歷史古蹟。

> *spend* + 時間 + (*in*) + *V-ing* 花…（時間）做
>
> *historic sites* 歷史古蹟

TEST 13

Directions: *Of the four choices given after each sentence, choose the one most suitable for filling in the blank.*

1. _____ stay indoors? It's raining outside.
   (A) Why
   (B) Why not
   (C) How about
   (D) How come ( )

2. Make sure that the sick _____ properly attended.
   (A) are
   (B) has
   (C) is
   (D) will have ( )

3. He told me his father was an astronaut, _____ was hard to believe.
   (A) it
   (B) that
   (C) what
   (D) which ( )

4. There was a sign at the lake, which said, "_____."
   (A) No fish
   (B) Not to fish
   (C) No fishing
   (D) Not fishing ( )

5. I wonder why Steven avoided _____ Kelly yesterday.
   (A) to meet
   (B) meeting
   (C) from meeting
   (D) having met ( )

6. _____ he be given another chance, he would make efforts to become a good student.

   (A) If
   (B) When
   (C) Might
   (D) Should   (   )

7. Are there any good films _____ this week?

   (A) about
   (B) by
   (C) on
   (D) out of   (   )

8. Her sister bought three _____ of stockings yesterday.

   (A) pieces
   (B) pairs
   (C) lumps
   (D) tubes   (   )

9. I was called into the office first, my name _____ at the head of the list.

   (A) holding
   (B) putting
   (C) making
   (D) being   (   )

10. Students should try _____ late.

    (A) not be
    (B) to not be
    (C) to don't be
    (D) not to be   (   )

TEST 13 詳解

1. (**B**) ***Why not*** stay indoors? It's raining outside.
   你為什麼不留在室內？外面正在下雨。

   「***Why not*** + 原形動詞」，形成疑問句。

   indoors〔'ın'dorz〕 *adv.* 在室內

2. (**A**) Make sure that ***the sick are*** properly attended.
   務必要使病人受到妥善的照顧。

   「***the*** + 形容詞 = 複數名詞」，故須用複數動詞，且依句意為被動，
   故選 (A)。(詳見文法寶典 p.192)
   the sick 病人 (= *sick people*)
   the rich 有錢人 (= *rich people*)
   the old 老人 (= *old people*)
   properly〔'prɑpəlı〕 *adv.* 適當地   attend〔ə'tɛnd〕 *v.* 照顧

3. (**D**) He told me *his father was an astronaut,* ***which*** *was hard to*
   believe. 他告訴我說，他的父親是太空人，真是令人難以相信。

   astronaut〔'æstrə,nɔt〕 *n.* 太空人

   關代 which 可代替前面一整句話，引導補述用法的形容詞子句。
   補述用法的形容詞子句不可用 that 引導，要用 which，而且前面
   必須有逗點。(詳見文法寶典 p.161,162)

4. (**C**) There was a sign at the lake, *which said,* "***No fishing.***"
   湖邊有張告示，上面寫著：「禁止釣魚。」

   「***No*** + ***V-ing.***」表「禁止」。如：***No parking.*** (禁止停車。)、
   No smoking. (禁止吸煙。)，***No fishing.*** (禁止釣魚。) 等。
   sign〔saın〕 *n.* 告示

5. (**B**) I wonder *why Steven* ***avoided*** ***meeting*** *Kelly yesterday.*
   我想知道為什麼史蒂芬昨天和凱莉避不見面。

   avoid + ***V-ing*** 避免

6. (**D**) **_Should he be_** _given another chance_, he would make efforts to become a good student.

如果能再給他一次機會，他會努力成為好學生的。

> 本句是由 _If he should be given another chance,_ … 轉化而來。
> If 被省略時，助動詞須置於主詞之前，形成倒裝。should 作「萬一」
> 解，表可能性極小的假設。　　**_make efforts to_** 努力

7. (**C**) Are there any good films **_on_** this week?

這星期有好看的電影上映嗎？

> **_on_** 在此為形容詞，作「上映中」解。
> 例如：What's on? (上演什麼電影？)
> film〔fɪlm〕*n.* 影片

8. (**B**) Her sister bought three <u>pairs</u> of stockings yesterday.

她妹妹昨天買了三雙長襪。

> **_a pair of stockings_** 一雙長襪　　stockings〔'stɑkɪŋz〕*n.pl.* 長襪
> a piece of advice 一個忠告
> a lump of sugar 一塊糖　　lump〔lʌmp〕*n.* 塊
> a tube of toothpaste 一條牙膏　　tube〔tjub〕*n.* 管狀物

9. (**D**) I was called into the office first, _my name being at the head of the list._

由於我的名字是名單上的第一個，所以最先被叫進辦公室。

> 本句是由…, _because my name was at the head of the list._
> 轉化而來。

10. (**D**) Students should **_try not to be_** late. 學生應該儘量不要遲到。

> ⎧ **_try to_** + *V*. 試著
> ⎩ **_try not to_** + *V*. 試著不要
> 不定詞的否定，否定的字須放在不定詞前面。

TEST 14

Directions: *Of the four choices given after each sentence, choose the one most suitable for filling in the blank.*

1. The old American didn't know that Singapore is a country _____ to the south of Malaysia.
   - (A) lain
   - (B) lying
   - (C) to lie
   - (D) which is lying   (   )

2. Honestly speaking, my income is _____ but as large as you think it is.
   - (A) nothing
   - (B) anything
   - (C) something
   - (D) everything   (   )

3. He _____ neglect his duty.
   - (A) ought to not
   - (B) ought not to
   - (C) ought not
   - (D) not ought to   (   )

4. _____ hearing the news, she burst into tears.
   - (A) Into
   - (B) On
   - (C) To
   - (D) At   (   )

5. _____ you speak about my husband in that disgusting way!
   - (A) What for
   - (B) How about
   - (C) How dare
   - (D) How would you say   (   )

6. Tony called on Mary _____ to find that she was away for the vacation.

    (A) as
    (B) until
    (C) only
    (D) before   (   )

7. If I _____ to college at that time, I would be a more successful businessman now.

    (A) go
    (B) went
    (C) have gone
    (D) had gone   (   )

8. _____ what to say, she remained silent.

    (A) Doesn't know
    (B) Knowing nothing
    (C) Not known
    (D) Not knowing   (   )

9. This is the place _____ I saw him last night.

    (A) that
    (B) which
    (C) what
    (D) where   (   )

10. Five kilometers _____ a long way if people have to walk.

    (A) are
    (B) is
    (C) was
    (D) were   (   )

TEST 14 詳解

1. (**B**) The old American didn't know *that Singapore is a country lying to the south of Malaysia.*

那位年老的美國人，不知道新加坡是位於馬來西亞南方的國家。

> 本句是由…*a country which lies to the south*…簡化而來。
> lie、lay 的三態變化及現在分詞爲：(如何背，見本書 p.16)
> | lie | lied | lied | lying | 說謊 |
> | *lie* | *lay* | *lain* | *lying* | 躺；位於 |
> | lay | laid | laid | laying | 放置 |

2. (**B**) *Honestly speaking*, my income is **anything but** *as* large *as you think it is.* 老實說，我的收入絕不如你所想的那麼高。

> income「收入」的多或少，須用 large 和 small 形容。
> | *anything but* 絕不 | *nothing but* 僅僅 | *all but* 幾乎 |
> | *= by no means* | *= only* | *= almost* |
> | *= not at all* | | |

3. (**B**) He **ought not to** neglect his duty. 他不該疏忽職守。

> | *ought to = should* 應該 |
> | *ought not to = should not* 不應該 |
> neglect〔nɪ'glɛkt〕*v.* 疏忽　　duty〔'djutɪ〕*n.* 本份；職責

4. (**B**) **On hearing the news**, she burst into tears.

一聽到這個消息，她就放聲大哭。

> *On + V-ing* 一…就 (*= As soon as* + 子句)
> *burst into tears* 突然大哭 (*= burst out crying*)

5. (**C**) **How dare you** speak about my husband *in that disgusting way*! 你竟敢用那種噁心的方式談論我的丈夫！

> *How dare you* + 原形 *V.* 你竟敢　dare 是助動詞。(詳見文法寶典 p.320)
> disgusting〔dɪs'gʌstɪŋ〕*adj.* 噁心的

6. (**C**) Tony called on Mary *only to find that she was away for the vacation.* 東尼去拜訪瑪麗，但卻發現她出門去渡假了。

　　　call on 拜訪（某人）

　　　不定詞片語修飾動詞，可表示目的、結果、原因等。但表示「令人失望的結果」，要用 ***only to*** + *V.*「結果卻」。

7. (**D**) *If I **had gone** to college at that time,* I **would be** a more successful businessman *now.*

　　　如果我當時有上大學，現在就會是個更成功的商人了。

　　　依句意，If 子句為「與過去事實相反的假設」，所以動詞用「過去完成式」，而主要子句為「與現在事實相反的假設」，動詞須用「should / would / could / might + 原形動詞」。

8. (**D**) *Not knowing what to say,* she remained silent.

　　　因為不知道說什麼，所以她就保持沉默。

　　　本句是由 *Because she did not know what to say,* …轉化而來。
　　　remain（rɪ'men）*v.* 保持　　silent（'saɪlənt）*adj.* 沉默的

9. (**D**) This is the place *where I saw him last night.*　完整的子句

　　　這就是我昨晚見到他的地方。

　　　關係副詞 where 和關係代名詞 which 與 that 都可以引導形容詞子句，而關係副詞 where 為純粹連接詞，無代名作用。where 在此相當於 at which。

10. (**B**) *Five kilometers **is** a long way *if people have to walk.*

　　　如果得用走的，五公里是一段很長的路程。

　　　***Five kilometers is** a long way,* …
　　　= ***The distance** of five kilometers **is** a long way,* …

　　　表示「一段距離」、「一段時間」、「一個重量」、「一筆金錢」的名詞，雖然形式上是複數，但意義上為單數，所以用單數動詞。

　　　（一定要看文法寶典 p.394）

TEST 15

Directions: *Of the four choices given after each sentence, choose the one most suitable for filling in the blank.*

1. Why on _____ did you sell your newly-built house?
   - (A) earth
   - (B) place
   - (C) reason
   - (D) ground ( )

2. Since he needed to sign the document, he asked me if I had anything _____.
   - (A) to write
   - (B) to write with
   - (C) to be written
   - (D) to writing on ( )

3. You are the _____ person I would have expected to see here.
   - (A) surprising
   - (B) rare
   - (C) least
   - (D) last ( )

4. Your cell phone is really small, _____ with mine.
   - (A) to compare
   - (B) comparing
   - (C) if compare
   - (D) compared ( )

5. Never _____ of meeting you here in Taipei.
   - (A) I dreamed
   - (B) did I dream
   - (C) dreamed I
   - (D) I did dream ( )

6. Although it was raining heavily this morning, the rain finally
   let _____ in the afternoon.

   (A) on
   (B) up
   (C) off
   (D) out   (   )

7. I'll have finished my homework by the time the TV
   program _____.

   (A) starts
   (B) will start
   (C) have started
   (D) will have started   (   )

8. She promised _____ the next chance go by.

   (A) not him to let
   (B) him not to let
   (C) him not letting
   (D) to him to let   (   )

9. There is no possibility of Mary _____ the bar exam.

   (A) to pass
   (B) passing
   (C) will pass
   (D) have passed   (   )

10. Scholars agree that the variety of wildlife is nowadays less
    than _____ used to be.

    (A) those
    (B) it
    (C) they
    (D) ones   (   )

TEST 15 詳解

1. (**A**) Why *on earth* did you sell your newly-built house?
你究竟爲什麼要把你剛蓋好的房子賣掉？

$$\begin{cases} \textit{on earth} & 究竟；到底（在疑問句中） \\ = \textit{in the world} \end{cases}$$

2. (**B**) *Since he needed to sign the document*, he asked me *if I had anything to write with*.
因爲他必須簽署文件，所以就問我，是否有任何可以拿來寫字的東西。

不定詞片語可當形容詞用，置於所修飾的名詞後面，而被修飾的名詞是不定詞意義上的受詞時，其介詞不可省，故選 (B)。（詳見文法寶典 P.412）
sign〔saɪn〕*v.* 簽名　　document〔'dɑkjəmənt〕*n.* 文件

3. (**D**) You are *the last* person *I would have expected to see here*.
眞沒想到會在這裏見到你。

「*the last* + *N*.」表「最不可能的」。
rare〔rɛr〕*adj.* 罕見的

4. (**D**) Your cell phone is really small, *compared with mine*.
和我的比起來，你的行動電話眞的很小。

本句是由…, *if your cell phone is compared with mine*. 轉化而來。compared with…常常使用，可當做慣用語來背。
cell phone 行動電話（= *cellular phone*）

5. (**B**) *Never did I dream* of meeting you *here in Taipei*.
我做夢也沒想到，會在台北這裏遇見你。

否定詞放句首，句子須倒裝，助動詞須置於主詞之前，選 (B)。

6. (**B**) *Although it was raining heavily this morning,* the rain finally ***let up*** in the afternoon.

雖然今天早上雨勢很大，但下午雨終於停了。

> 依句意，選 (B) *let up*「停止」。而 (A) let on「洩漏」，(C) let off「放（煙火）」，(D) let out「放出」，則不合句意。

7. (**A**) I'll have finished my homework ***by the time*** *the TV program starts.* 電視節目開始之前，我就把功課做完了。

> 表時間或條件的副詞子句，須用現在式表未來，故選 (A)。

8. (**B**) She promised <u>him not to let</u> the next chance go by.

她向他保證，不會讓下次的機會溜走。

> $\begin{cases} \textit{promise sb. to} + V. \text{ 向某人保證會} \\ \textit{promise sb. not to} + V. \text{ 向某人保證不會} \end{cases}$
>
> ***go by*** 錯過

9. (**B**) There is no possibility *of Mary passing* the bar exam.

瑪麗不可能通過律師考試。

> Mary 是動名詞 passing 意義上的主詞。Mary passing 做介系詞 of 的受詞，此時 Mary 也可用所有格的形式 Mary's。（詳見文法寶典 p.426）

10. (**B**) Scholars agree *that* ***the variety*** of wildlife is *nowadays less than* ***it*** *used to be.*

學者都認為，現在野生動植物的種類，比以前少。

> variety 為單數名詞，故代名詞須用 it。本句相當於…*less than the variety of wildlife used to be.*
>
> variety〔vəˋraɪətɪ〕 *n.* 種類
>
> wildlife〔ˋwaɪldˏlaɪf〕 *n.* 野生動植物

TEST 16

Directions: *Of the four choices given after each sentence, choose the one most suitable for filling in the blank.*

1. _____ Michael looks tired; he stayed up all night.
   (A) There is wonder
   (B) It's no wonder
   (C) It's the reason for
   (D) This is reasonable   (　)

2. What do you say _____ a visit to the Palace Museum?
   (A) to pay
   (B) paying
   (C) to paying
   (D) having   (　)

3. _____ you have to do is sit down and stay calm.
   (A) All
   (B) Only
   (C) How
   (D) Which   (　)

4. He saw a girl _____ in blue.
   (A) dressed
   (B) dressing
   (C) being dressed
   (D) dressed herself   (　)

5. There is no mother but _____ her children.
   (A) loves
   (B) love
   (C) loving
   (D) loved   (　)

6. The shopkeeper was busy _____ the customer and didn't notice that the boy was about to shoplift.

    (A) serving
    (B) to serve
    (C) to serve to
    (D) with serving   (   )

7. This is the very book _____ I wanted to buy.

    (A) that
    (B) what
    (C) how
    (D) when   (   )

8. Though he has a Ph.D. in archaeology, he is not _____ of an archaeologist.

    (A) more
    (B) much
    (C) less
    (D) little   (   )

9. The teacher had hardly finished the class _____ Jimmy rushed out of the classroom.

    (A) after
    (B) when
    (C) as
    (D) where   (   )

10. Cindy was made _____ all the dishes after the dinner.

    (A) wash
    (B) washed
    (C) washing
    (D) to wash   (   )

TEST 16 詳解

1. (**B**) ***It's no wonder*** *Michael looks tired*; he stayed up all night.
難怪麥可看起來很累；他整晚沒睡。

$$\begin{cases} \textit{It is no wonder (that)} \sim & 難怪 \\ = \textit{No wonder (that)} \sim \end{cases}$$

而 (C) for 爲介系詞，不可接子句；(D) 動詞 is 與 looks 之間，缺少連接詞，不合文法。　　***stay up*** 熬夜

2. (**C**) ***What do you say to paying*** a visit to the Palace Museum?
去參觀故宮博物院，你覺得怎麼樣？

palace〔'pælɪs 〕*n.* 皇宮

$$\begin{cases} \textit{What do you say to} + \textit{V-ing} & \sim 怎麼樣？（注意：to是介系詞） \\ = \textit{How about} + \textit{V-ing} \\ = \textit{What about} + \textit{V-ing} \end{cases}$$

3. (**A**) ***All you have to do*** *is* sit down and stay calm.
你所必須做的，就是坐下來，並保持冷靜。

All one has to do is (to) + ***V*** 某人所必須做的是
這條題目常考，因爲有三個動詞在一起。

4. (**A**) He saw a girl *dressed in blue.* 他看見一個穿藍色衣服的女孩。

本句是由 *He saw a girl who was dressed in blue.* 簡化而來。

$$\begin{cases} \textit{be dressed in} & 穿著（衣服） \\ = \textit{dress oneself in} \end{cases}$$

5. (**A**) There is *no* mother *but loves* her children.
沒有母親不愛自己的子女。

but 前有否定字，but 本身又有否定意義，形成雙重否定時，要用準關代 but，引導形容詞子句（詳見文法寶典 p.160）。整句話表示不變的事實，動詞要用現在式。but 代替 mother，是單數，故用單數動詞。

6. (**A**) The shopkeeper *was busy serving* the customer and didn't notice *that the boy was about to shoplift.*

商店老板忙著服務客人，沒注意到那個小男孩正要順手牽羊。

$\begin{cases} \textbf{\textit{be busy (in)}} + \textbf{\textit{V-ing}} \ 忙於 \\ = \textbf{\textit{be busy with}} + \textbf{\textit{N.}} \end{cases}$

be about to 正要　　shoplift (ˈʃɑpˌlɪft) *v.* 順手牽羊

7. (**A**) This is ***the very*** book *that I wanted to buy.*

這正是我想買的那本書。

very (ˈvɛrɪ) *adj.* 正是；就是 (加強名詞的語氣)

先行詞之前有 the only, the same, the very, the first, the last, 或 all, only, any, no, every 的時候，關代常用 that。

8. (**B**) *Though he has a Ph.D. in archaeology,* he is *not much of an* archaeologist.

雖然他有人類學的博士學位，但他並不是什麼了不起的人類學家。

not much of a(n) 不是什麼了不起的

archaeology (ˌɑrkɪˈɑlədʒɪ) *n.* 人類學

9. (**B**) The teacher had ***hardly*** finished the class *when Jimmy rushed out of the classroom.* 老師一上完課，吉米就衝出教室。

$S + had + \begin{cases} \textbf{\textit{hardly}} \\ \textbf{\textit{scarcely}} \end{cases} + \text{p.p.} + \begin{cases} \textbf{\textit{when}} \\ \textbf{\textit{before}} \end{cases} + S. + 過去式 V.$
　　　　　一…就

10. (**D**) Cindy *was made to wash* all the dishes after the dinner.

辛蒂在吃完晚餐後，被叫去洗所有的碗。

make 為使役動詞，其被動語態，不定詞的 to 須保留。

be made to V. 被叫去

TEST 17

Directions: *Of the four choices given after each sentence, choose the one most suitable for filling in the blank.*

1. It will be _____ spring when you get to London.
   - (A) late
   - (B) lately
   - (C) last
   - (D) latest   (   )

2. He was very nervous because he _____ in public.
   - (A) didn't use to speak
   - (B) didn't used to speak
   - (C) wasn't used to speaking
   - (D) wasn't used to speak   (   )

3. She does not seem to be _____ of guessing others' feelings.
   - (A) enabled
   - (B) possible
   - (C) able
   - (D) capable   (   )

4. _____ this letter find you well and happy!
   - (A) I am afraid
   - (B) I think
   - (C) May
   - (D) Will   (   )

5. If I were _____ go abroad, I would go to France.
   - (A) on
   - (B) to
   - (C) about
   - (D) for   (   )

6. I remember _____ him at this place two years ago.

    (A) to see
    (B) seeing
    (C) to seeing
    (D) to be seen   (   )

7. It was stupid _____ him to say such a thing to the teacher.

    (A) with
    (B) of
    (C) as
    (D) to   (   )

8. Although intonation is seldom taught in some language courses, it is _____ important for communicating accurately.

    (A) all the more
    (B) none the less
    (C) none the worse
    (D) much more   (   )

9. It _____ him millions of dollars to buy the villa in the countryside.

    (A) spent
    (B) cost
    (C) took
    (D) made   (   )

10. You _____ go to bed as stay up doing nothing.

    (A) should
    (B) had better
    (C) would rather
    (D) might as well   (   )

TEST 17 詳解

1. (**A**) It will be ***late spring*** *when you get to London*.
　　你到達倫敦時，就是暮春了。

　　　依句意，選 (A) ***late spring*** 「晚春；暮春」。又如 in the late nineteenth century，則表「在十九世紀末」。

2. (**C**) He was *very* nervous *because he **wasn't used to speaking in public**.* 他很緊張，因為他不習慣在衆人面前說話。

$\begin{cases} \textbf{\textit{used to}} + \text{原形 } V. \text{ 從前} \\ \textbf{\textit{be used to}} + \textbf{\textit{V-ing}} \text{ 習慣於} \end{cases}$ 　nervous〔'nɝvəs〕*adj.* 緊張的

3. (**D**) She does not seem to ***be capable of*** guessing others' feelings.
　　她似乎無法猜出別人的感受。

$\begin{cases} \textbf{\textit{be capable of}} + \textbf{\textit{V-ing}} \text{ 能夠} \\ = \textbf{\textit{be able to}} + V. \end{cases}$

　　　而 (A) enable + 人 + to V. 「使某人能夠」，用法不合。
　　　(B) possible 「可能的」，爲「非人稱形容詞」，不能以人當主詞。

4. (**C**) ***May*** this letter find you well and happy!
　　但願這封信寄給你時，你旣健康又快樂！

　　　「May + S. + 原形 V.」表「祝福」。

5. (**B**) *If I **were to go abroad**,* I *would go* to France.
　　如果我出國的話，我會去法國。

　　　表「與未來事實相反的假設」，其公式爲：

$$\text{If} + S. + \begin{cases} \textbf{\textit{were to}} + V. \\ \text{過去式 } V. \end{cases}, \quad S. + \begin{cases} \textbf{\textit{should}} \\ \textbf{\textit{would}} \\ \textbf{\textit{could}} \\ \textbf{\textit{might}} \end{cases} + V.$$

6. (**B**) I *remember* *seeing* him *at this place two years ago.*
我記得兩年前在這個地方見過他。

$\begin{cases} \textit{remember} + \textit{V-ing} \ \text{記得曾 (動作已完成)} \\ \textit{remember} + \textit{to V.} \ \text{記得要去 (動作未完成)} \end{cases}$

7. (**B**) It was stupid *of* him to say such a thing to the teacher.
他真笨，竟向老師說這樣的事。

$\begin{cases} \text{It is} + \text{褒貶的形容詞 (描寫人)} + \text{of} + \text{人} + \text{to V.} \\ \text{It is} + \text{非人稱形容詞 (描寫事)} + \text{for} + \text{人} + \text{to V.} \end{cases}$

8. (**B**) *Although intonation is seldom taught in some language*

courses, it is *none the less* important for communicating

accurately. 雖然有些語言課程很少教語調，但要正確地溝通，語調仍
然是很重要的。

none the less 仍然 (none 等於 not at all，「一點都不少於」，即表「仍然」)
all the more 更加　　intonation〔͵ɪntoˈneʃən〕*n.* 音調；語調

9. (**B**) It *cost* him millions of dollars *to buy the villa in the*

countryside. 他花了好幾百萬元，在鄉間買了一棟別墅。

「物 + cost + 人 + 錢」表「某物花了某人 (錢)」。
「人 + spend + 錢」表「某人花了 (錢)」。
villa〔ˈvɪlə〕*n.* 別墅　　countryside〔ˈkʌntrɪ͵saɪd〕*n.* 鄉間

10. (**D**) You *might as well* go to bed *as* stay up doing nothing.
最好睡覺去好了，不要熬夜不做事。

$\begin{cases} \textit{might as well} + \text{原形 V.} + \textit{as} + \text{原形 V.} \ \text{最好…不要} \\ = \textit{had better} + \text{原形 V.} + \textit{than} + \text{原形 V.} \end{cases}$

might as well 是助動詞的慣用語，常考。(詳見文法寶典 p.317)
stay up 熬夜

TEST 18

Directions: *Of the four choices given after each sentence, choose the one most suitable for filling in the blank.*

1. We are different _____ that you like crowds and I don't.

   (A) so
   (B) of
   (C) at
   (D) in   (   )

2. I would rather _____ at home myself than eat out.

   (A) cook
   (B) cooking
   (C) to cook
   (D) to cooking   (   )

3. Tom has _____ for modern painting.

   (A) an eye
   (B) the eye
   (C) eyes
   (D) the eyes   (   )

4. Rome is a city worth _____.

   (A) visit
   (B) to visit
   (C) visiting
   (D) to visiting   (   )

5. If only you _____ to the movies with me last night!

   (A) would go
   (B) went
   (C) had gone
   (D) go   (   )

6. How come _____ such a lie?

    (A) he told
    (B) did he tell
    (C) has he told
    (D) was he to tell   (   )

7. We regret _____ you that you are to be dismissed next week.

    (A) tell
    (B) to tell
    (C) told
    (D) to telling   (   )

8. He used to _____ to school every morning.

    (A) walk
    (B) walking
    (C) being walked
    (D) having walked   (   )

9. I saw a beautiful lady sitting with her legs _____.

    (A) crosses
    (B) crossed
    (C) crossing
    (D) to cross   (   )

10. _____, he could speak confidently in public.

    (A) Being mere child
    (B) Mere child as he was
    (C) A mere child as he was
    (D) Though he was mere child   (   )

TEST 18 詳解

1.(**D**) We are different *in that* you like crowds and I don't.
我們不一樣，因為你喜歡人群，而我不喜歡。

> $\begin{cases} \textbf{\textit{in that}} \ \text{因為（that 子句不可做介系詞的受詞，但 in that 例外。）} \\ = \textbf{\textit{because}} \end{cases}$

2.(**A**) I *would rather* <u>cook</u> at home myself *than* eat out.
我寧願自己在家煮，也不願出去外面吃。

> 「*would rather* + *V.*…*than* + *V.*」，表「寧願…，也不願」。

3.(**A**) Tom *has* <u>*an eye*</u> *for* modern painting.
湯姆懂得欣賞現代畫。

> *have an eye for* 懂得欣賞（這是慣用語，不可說成 *have the eye for*。）

4.(**C**) Rome is a city *worth* <u>*visiting*</u>.
羅馬是個值得一遊的城市。

> *be worth* + *V-ing* 值得
> （動名詞必須是主動的，必須是及物動詞，但無受詞。）
> worth 是少數可接受詞的形容詞。

5.(**C**) *If only* you <u>*had gone*</u> to the movies with me last night!
要是你昨晚和我一起去看電影，不知道有多好！

> 「*If only*…」表「不可能實現的願望」，作「但願；要是…不知
> 該有多好」解。
>
> $\begin{cases} \textbf{\textit{If only}} \\ = \textbf{\textit{I wish}} \end{cases} + \text{S.} + \begin{cases} \textbf{\textit{were}} \ \text{或過去式動詞（與現在事實相反）} \\ \textbf{\textit{had}} + \textbf{\textit{p.p.}} \ \text{（與過去事實相反）} \\ \text{過去式助動詞} + \textbf{\textit{V.}} \ \text{（與未來事實相反）} \end{cases}$
>
> 依句意，為「與過去事實相反的願望」，動詞用過去完成式，選 (C)。

6. (**A**) *How come he told such a lie?*
他為什麼會說這樣的謊？

> *How come* + 子句，形成疑問句。
> = *How did it come that…?*

7. (**B**) We *regret to tell* you *that you are to be dismissed next week.*
我們很遺憾要告訴你，下週起你將被解僱。　dismiss〔dɪsˋmɪs〕v. 解僱

> ⎰ *regret* + *to V.* 很遺憾要
> ⎱ *regret* + *V-ing* 後悔曾

8. (**A**) He *used to walk* to school every morning.
他從前每天早上走路去上學。

> ⎰ *used to* + *V.* 從前
> ⎱ *be used to* + *V-ing* 習慣於

9. (**B**) I saw a beautiful lady *sitting with her legs crossed*.
我看見一位美女雙腳交叉地坐著。　　cross〔krɔs〕v. 交叉

> 「*with* + 受詞 + 分詞」表示「伴隨著主要動詞的情況」，受詞是「人」
> 用現在分詞，「非人」用過去分詞。一般文法書中，人做主詞，用主
> 動，物作主詞，用被動，是錯誤的觀念，應該把「物」改成「非人」，
> 如眼睛、手、腳等，都是「非人」。(詳見文法寶典 p.462)

10. (**B**) *Mere child as he was*, he could speak confidently in public.
雖然他只是個孩子，他卻能在眾人面前，很有自信地說話。

> as 用於表讓步的副詞子句，有下列幾種型式：
>
> ⎧ 名詞 (無冠詞) ⎫
> ⎪ 形容詞 　　 ⎪ + as + 主詞 + 動詞
> ⎨ 副　詞 　　 ⎬ (詳見文法寶典 p.529)
> ⎩ 分　詞 　　 ⎭
>
> Mere child *as* he was, …
> = *Although* he was a mere child, …
> mere〔mɪr〕adj. 僅僅；只是

TEST 19

Directions: *Of the four choices given after each sentence, choose the one most suitable for filling in the blank.*

1. Relax. The angrier you get, _____ you become.
   - (A) the uglier
   - (B) more ugly
   - (C) ugly person
   - (D) the more ugly   (   )

2. You should know _____ than to lend him money. He will never repay you.
   - (A) best
   - (B) better
   - (C) well
   - (D) fine   (   )

3. My mother insisted _____ up smoking.
   - (A) me giving
   - (B) I gave
   - (C) on my giving
   - (D) on I should give   (   )

4. The question is which _____.
   - (A) choose
   - (B) to choose
   - (C) choosing
   - (D) chosen   (   )

5. _____ you have formed a bad habit, it is difficult to get rid of it.
   - (A) Until
   - (B) Unless
   - (C) Before
   - (D) Once   (   )

6. They are so _____ that it is difficult to tell which is which.

    (A) alike
    (B) likely
    (C) nearly
    (D) same   (   )

7. It _____ me two hours to find your new house.

    (A) cost
    (B) took
    (C) spent
    (D) occupied   (   )

8. Roughly _____, this is correct.

    (A) speak
    (B) spoke
    (C) speaking
    (D) to speak   (   )

9. He _____ sometimes go mountain-climbing with his friends when young.

    (A) used
    (B) should
    (C) would
    (D) is used to   (   )

10. Such _____ the case, I can't let you go.

    (A) is
    (B) doing
    (C) being
    (D) done   (   )

TEST 19 詳解

1. (**A**) Relax. *The angrier* you get, *the uglier you become.*
放輕鬆。你愈生氣，就變得愈醜。

  「the + 比較級，the + 比較級」表「愈…，就愈…」。
  形容詞 ugly「醜的」，比較級是 uglier，不是 *more ugly*。

2. (**B**) You should *know better than to* lend him money. He will never repay you.
你應該不致於笨到把錢借給他。他不會還給你的。

  know better than to V. 不致於笨到去

3. (**C**) My mother *insisted on* my giving up smoking.
我媽媽堅持要我戒煙。

  $\begin{cases} \textit{insist on} + (\textit{one's}) + \textit{V-ing} \text{ 堅持} \\ \textit{insist that} + S. + (\textit{should}) + V. \end{cases}$

4. (**B**) The question is *which to choose.*
問題是該選哪一個。

  「疑問詞 + *to V.*」形成名詞片語。
  本句中的 which to choose 做主詞 question 的補語。

5. (**D**) *Once you have formed a bad habit*, it is difficult to get rid of it. 一旦養成了壞習慣，就很難戒除了。

  once「一旦」為表時間或條件的連接詞，引導副詞子句，修飾動詞 is。
  form〔form〕v. 養成
  get rid of 擺脫；除去

6. (**A**) They are *so **alike** that it is difficult to tell which is which.*
　　他們非常相像，很難分辨哪一個是哪一個。

　　　依句意，選 (A) ***alike*** 〔 ə'laɪk 〕 *adj.* 相像的。而 (B) likely「可能的」，
　　　(C) nearly「幾乎」，不合句意。(D) same「同樣的」，前面須加 the，
　　　用法不合。
　　　tell 〔 tɛl 〕 *v.* 分辨

7. (**B**) It ***took*** me two hours *to find your new house.*
　　我花了兩小時才找到你的新房子。

　　　「It + ***takes*** + 人 + 時間 + ***to V.***」表「某事花某人多久時間」。
　　　(spend, take, cost 的用法，詳見文法寶典 p.299)

8. (**C**) ***Roughly speaking***, this is correct.
　　大致說來，這是正確的。

　　　roughly speaking 大致說來　　　roughly 〔 'rʌflɪ 〕 *adv.* 大約；粗略地
　　　其他類似的用法還有：frankly speaking「坦白說」，及 generally
　　　speaking「一般說來」等。(獨立分詞片語，詳見文法寶典 p.463)

9. (**C**) He ***would*** sometimes go mountain-climbing *with his friends*

　　when young. 他年輕時，有時會和朋友一起去爬山。

　　　助動詞 ***would*** 可表「過去的習慣」。(詳見文法寶典 p.309, 324)
　　　when young 是由 when he was young 簡化而來。

10. (**C**) ***Such being the case***, I can't let you go.
　　既然如此，我不能讓你走。

　　　such being the case 既然如此
　　　若選 (A) is，則兩子句之間無連接詞。
　　　本句是由：If such is the case, …轉化而來。

TEST 20

Directions: *Of the four choices given after each sentence, choose the one most suitable for filling in the blank.*

1. I was so _____ that I fell asleep before the film ended.
   - (A) bored
   - (B) boring
   - (C) bore
   - (D) boredom   (　)

2. It is necessary _____ the traffic rules.
   - (A) you following
   - (B) your following
   - (C) of you to follow
   - (D) for you to follow   (　)

3. Please write in ink, and don't forget to write _____ every other line.
   - (A) at
   - (B) from
   - (C) in
   - (D) on   (　)

4. The new medicine saved me from an illness which might _____ have been fatal.
   - (A) therefore
   - (B) still
   - (C) otherwise
   - (D) instead   (　)

5. Both of them are very brilliant, but _____ warm-hearted.
   - (A) neither of them is
   - (B) neither one of them are
   - (C) none of them is
   - (D) none of them are   (　)

6. _____ the air conditioner, the summertime would be unbearable.
   (A) Were it for
   (B) If it were not
   (C) If were it not
   (D) Were it not for   (   )

7. There are two reasons for our decision, and you know one of them. Now I'll tell you _____.
   (A) another
   (B) other
   (C) the other
   (D) the others   (   )

8. The doctor gave me _____ on how to keep fit.
   (A) much advices
   (B) many advices
   (C) a few advice
   (D) a great deal of advice   (   )

9. Please lock the door when you _____.
   (A) leave
   (B) will be leaving
   (C) will have left
   (D) will leave   (   )

10. Of these two opinions, I prefer the _____ to the former.
    (A) late
    (B) last
    (C) later
    (D) latter   (   )

TEST 20 詳解

1. (**A**) I was *so* <u>bored</u> *that I fell asleep before the film ended.*
   我覺得很無聊，所以電影結束前，就睡著了。

   > 情感動詞，「人」做主詞用過去分詞，「非人」做主詞，用現在分詞。
   >
   > 例：
   > - It interests me. (它使我有興趣。)
   > - = I'm interested in it. (我對它有興趣。)
   > - = It is interesting to me. (它令我有興趣。)
   >
   > bore 是情感動詞，故選 (A)。(詳見文法寶典 p.389,390)

2. (**D**) It is necessary *for you to follow* the traffic rules.
   你必須遵守交通規則。

   > 「It is + 非人稱形容詞 + *for* + 人 + to V.」表「對某人而言」。
   > follow〔'fɑlo〕*v.* 遵守   *traffic rules* 交通規則

3. (**D**) Please write in ink, and don't forget to write *on every other line*. 請用墨水寫，而且不要忘了隔行寫。

   > *on a line* 在一條線上   *on every other line* 在每隔一條線上

4. (**C**) The new medicine saved me from an illness *which might otherwise have been fatal.*
   這種新藥治好了我的病，否則這種病可能會要了我的命。

   > 依句意，選 (C) *otherwise*「否則」。otherwise 代替一個 if 子句。(詳見文法寶典 p.367, 474) 而 (A) 因此，(B) 仍然，(D) 相反地，則不合句意。
   > fatal〔'fetḷ〕*adj.* 致命的

5. (**A**) Both of them are very brilliant, but *neither of them is* warm-hearted. 他們兩個人都非常聰明，但是沒有一個是熱心的。

   > 表「兩者皆不」，用 neither，且 neither 為單數代名詞，故選 (A)。
   > brilliant〔'brɪlɪənt〕*adj.* 聰明的
   > warm-hearted〔'wɔrm'hɑrtɪd〕*adj.* 熱心的；有同情心的

6. (**D**) ‾‾‾‾‾‾‾‾‾‾‾‾‾‾‾‾‾‾‾‾‾‾‾‾‾
Were it not for the air conditioner, the summertime *would* be unbearable. 要不是有冷氣機，夏天眞是令人無法忍受。

  { Were it not for 要不是 (表與現在事實相反的假設)
   = If it were not for

  air conditioner 冷氣機 unbearable〔ʌn'bɛrəbḷ〕*adj.* 不可忍受的

7. (**C**) There are two reasons *for our decision*, and you know *one* of them. Now I'll tell you *the other*.
我們做這樣的決定有兩個理由，而其中一個你已經知道了。現在我就把另一個理由告訴你。

  只有兩者的情況，一個用 one，另一個用 *the other*。
  而 (A) another 指「(三者以上) 另一個」，(B) other「其他的」，
  (D) the others「另外的那些」，均不合句意。

8. (**D**) The doctor gave me *a great deal of advice* *on how to keep fit.* 醫生給我許多如何保持健康的建議。 fit〔fit〕*adj.* 健康的
  advice「建議；忠告」是抽象名詞，不可數，字尾不可加 S，也不可
  用 *many* 或 *a few* 修飾，故選 (D) *a great deal of advice*「很多忠告」
  (= *much advice*)。
  抽象名詞和物質名詞，可用單位名詞表「數」的觀念。如 a piece of
  advice「一個忠告」。(詳見文法寶典 p.69)

9. (**A**) Please lock the door *when you leave*. 離開時，請把門鎖上。
  表時間的副詞子句，不可用 shall 或 will 表未來，須用現在式表未來。
  lock〔lɑk〕*v.* 鎖

10. (**D**) *Of these two opinions*, I prefer *the latter* to *the former*.
在這兩個意見中，我比較喜歡後者，比較不喜歡前者。

  the former 前者 *the latter* 後者
  而 (A) late「遲到的」，(B) last「最後的」，(C) later「後來」，則不
  合句意。 *prefer* A *to* B 比較喜歡 A，比較不喜歡 B

TEST 21

Directions: *Of the four choices given after each sentence, choose the one most suitable for filling in the blank.*

1. She has to study _____ two years before she graduates.
   - (A) more
   - (B) another
   - (C) other
   - (D) much ( )

2. Mary didn't want to walk at night on her own _____ something terrible should happen to her.
   - (A) so that
   - (B) unless
   - (C) despite the fact that
   - (D) for fear that ( )

3. I know nothing about Roy _____ he is a college student.
   - (A) excepting
   - (B) except for
   - (C) except from
   - (D) except that ( )

4. The doctor is a great authority _____ children's diseases.
   - (A) on
   - (B) in
   - (C) of
   - (D) over ( )

5. If they had surrendered, we _____ them.
   - (A) shouldn't kill
   - (B) needed not to kill
   - (C) didn't have killed
   - (D) needn't have killed ( )

6. The discussion the villagers had on the environment was quite _____.

    (A) alive
    (B) lived
    (C) lively
    (D) living   (   )

7. My father objected to _____ like an invalid.

    (A) treat
    (B) treating
    (C) be treated
    (D) being treated   (   )

8. I don't know _____ to consult with.

    (A) what
    (B) when
    (C) where
    (D) whom   (   )

9. As the French enjoy their wine, _____ the Chinese enjoy their tea.

    (A) as
    (B) so
    (C) such
    (D) like   (   )

10. A: Does Jack live in the suburbs or in the center of the city?
    B: _____ I know, he lives near the center.

    (A) As far as
    (B) As long as
    (C) As much as
    (D) So long as   (   )

TEST 21 詳解

1. (**B**) She has to study *another two years* before she graduates.
她必須再唸兩年才能畢業。

> $\begin{cases} \textbf{\textit{another two years}} \ 再兩年 \\ = \textbf{\textit{two more years}} \end{cases}$　　graduate〔'grædʒʊ,et〕*v.* 畢業

2. (**D**) Mary didn't want to walk *at night on her own* **for fear that** *something terrible* **should** *happen to her.*
瑪麗不想晚上一個人走，惟恐會有可怕的事發生在她身上。

> $\begin{cases} \textbf{\textit{for fear that}} \\ \textbf{\textit{lest}} \\ \textbf{\textit{in case (that)}} \end{cases}$ + S. + (*should*) + V. 以免；惟恐（表否定目的）

> *on one's own* 獨力；獨自；憑自己

3. (**D**) I know nothing about Roy *except that* he is a college student.
除了知道羅伊是個大學生之外，其他我一無所知。

> *except that* + 子句　除了～之外

4. (**A**) The doctor is a great authority *on children's diseases.*
那位醫生是兒童疾病方面的權威。

> 介系詞 *on* 表「關於～方面」。（詳見文法寶典 p. 593）
> authority〔ə'θɔrətɪ〕*n.* 權威

5. (**D**) *If they had surrendered,* we *needn't have killed* them.
如果當初他們投降的話，我們就不必殺死他們了。

> *needn't have* + *p.p.* 表「不必」（但已做）。（詳見文法寶典 p.322）
> *didn't need to* + *V.* 表「不必」（未做）。
> surrender〔sə'rɛndə〕*v.* 投降

6. (**C**) The discussion *the villagers had on the environment* was quite ___*lively*___. 村民對環境問題的討論十分熱烈。

依句意，選 (C) *lively* (ˋlaɪvlɪ) *adj.* 活潑的；熱烈的。
而 (A) alive (əˋlaɪv) *adj.* 活著的，則不合句意。
villager (ˋvɪlɪdʒɚ) *n.* 村民

7. (**D**) My father *objected to* being treated like an invalid.
我父親反對被當作病人來對待。

object to + $\begin{cases} \text{N.} \\ \text{V-ing} \end{cases}$ 「反對」，to 為介系詞，且依句意為被動，

故選 (D)。　　invalid (ˋɪnvəlɪd) *n.* 病人

8. (**D**) I don't know ___*whom to consult with*___.
我不知道該請教誰。　consult (kənˋsʌlt) *v.* 請教

「疑問詞＋不定詞」形成「名詞片語」。疑問代名詞 whom 做 with 的受詞。
本句等於 I don't know *whom I should consult with.*

9. (**B**) *As the French enjoy their wine*, __*so*__ the Chinese enjoy their tea.
中國人喜歡喝茶，就像法國人喜歡喝酒一樣。

「*As~so* …」，表「…，就像～一樣」。這句話應該從後面開始翻譯。
例如：As you sow, so will you reap. (種瓜得瓜，種豆得豆。)
(一定要看文法寶典 p.502)

10. (**A**) A: Does Jack live *in the suburbs or in the center of the city*?
B: ___*As far as I know*___, he lives *near the center*.
甲：傑克是住在郊區還是市中心？
乙：據我所知，他住在市中心附近。

依句意，選 (A) *as far as I know*「據我所知」。而 (B) as long as
「只要」(= *so long as*)，(C) as much as「多達」，皆不合句意。
in the suburbs 在郊區 (= *on the outskirts*)

TEST 22

Directions: *Of the four choices given after each sentence, choose the one most suitable for filling in the blank.*

1. The sun rises _____ the east.
   - (A) to
   - (B) in
   - (C) at
   - (D) under   (   )

2. _____ you were a singer, what kind of song would you like to sing?
   - (A) Suppose
   - (B) Supposed
   - (C) Supposition
   - (D) Supposedly   (   )

3. It is a pity that nobody was saved in the accident, _____ it?
   - (A) does
   - (B) doesn't
   - (C) was
   - (D) isn't   (   )

4. The _____ fans rushed onto the stage during the concert.
   - (A) excite
   - (B) excited
   - (C) exciting
   - (D) excitement   (   )

5. Nancy studied hard _____ flunk calculus again.
   - (A) so as to
   - (B) as not to
   - (C) so as not to
   - (D) not so as to   (   )

6. He didn't come to work for some reason or _____.

    (A) other
    (B) another
    (C) others
    (D) the other   (   )

7. Charles has _____ better days and finds it difficult to live only on his pension.

    (A) removed
    (B) known
    (C) reminded
    (D) thought   (   )

8. As soon as he entered the village, he found himself _____ curious children.

    (A) surrounding
    (B) surrounded by
    (C) surrounding by
    (D) to be surrounding   (   )

9. We considered _____ but finally decided against it.

    (A) go
    (B) to go
    (C) going
    (D) about to go   (   )

10. Jane decided _____ the man she met in Paris.

    (A) to marry
    (B) marrying to
    (C) to marry with
    (D) to get married   (   )

TEST 22 詳解

1. (**B**) The sun rises ***in the east***. 太陽從東邊升起。

> 表示「方向」，介系詞用 *in*。(詳見文法寶典 p.579)
> 例：***In which direction*** did he go？(他朝哪個方向去了？)

2. (**A**) ***Suppose*** *you were a singer*, what kind of song would you like to sing? 如果你是歌手，你會想唱哪一種歌？

> *suppose* 如果 (不可説成 *supposed*)
> = *supposing* (要特別注意：原形動詞 *suppose*，過去分詞 *provided*，
> = *providing* 　居然都可當連接詞。)
> = *provided*
> = *if* (詳見文法寶典 p.456)

3. (**D**) It is a pity ***that*** *nobody was saved in the accident*, ***isn't it***?
那場意外中沒有人獲救，真是可惜，對不對？

> 附加問句是以主要思想爲主，是一個簡單形式的省略疑問句。
> *isn't it*? 是 *isn't it a pity*? 的省略。(詳見文法寶典 p.6)

4. (**B**) The ***excited*** fans rushed onto the stage *during the concert*.
演唱會中，有些興奮的歌迷衝上了舞台。

> 表示情感的動詞，須以其現在分詞修飾事物，過去分詞修飾人，故選
> (B) *excited*「興奮的」。
> fan〔fæn〕*n.* 歌迷　　rush〔rʌʃ〕*v.* 衝

5. (**C**) Nancy studied hard ***so as not to*** *flunk calculus again*.
南茜很用功，以免微積分又考不及格。

> *so as not to V.* 以免 (表否定目的)
> = *in order not to V.*
> flunk〔flʌŋk〕*v.* 不及格　　calculus〔ˈkælkjələs〕*n.* 微積分

6. (**A**) He didn't come to work *for some reason or other*.

他因爲某種原因，沒來上班。

    some…or other 某種；某些（some 之後可接單數或複數名詞）

    one…or another 某種；種種

7. (**B**) Charles has ___**known** better days___ and finds it difficult to live *only on his pension*.

查爾斯曾經風光一時，所以覺得很難只靠退休金生活。

    know better days 經歷鼎盛時期；風光一時

    live on 以～爲生   pension〔'pɛnʃən〕*n.* 退休金

8. (**B**) *As soon as he entered the village*, he **found** himself **surrounded by** curious children.

當他一進到村子裏，就發現自己被好奇的小孩包圍。

$$\text{find} + 受詞 + \begin{cases} 形容詞（表狀態） \\ \text{V-ing}（表主動） \\ \text{p.p.}（表被動） \end{cases}$$

    依句意，「被好奇的小孩包圍」，故選 (B) *surrounded by*。

9. (**C**) We ***considered going*** but *finally* decided against it.

我們考慮要去，但最後決定不去了。

    consider + V-ing 考慮   against〔ə'gɛnst〕*prep.* 反對

10. (**A**) Jane decided to marry the man *she met in Paris*.

珍決定要嫁給她在巴黎認識的那個人。

    decide to + V. 決定

    $\begin{cases} \textit{marry sb.} \ 和某人結婚 \\ = \textit{get married to sb.} \\ = \textit{be married to sb.} \end{cases}$

    （不可說成 *get married with sb.*）（詳見文法寶典 p.389）

TEST 23

Directions: *Of the four choices given after each sentence, choose the one most suitable for filling in the blank.*

1. He was _____ to give me a ride home.
   - (A) as kind
   - (B) more kind
   - (C) so kind as
   - (D) enough kind   (   )

2. All _____ there were some 250 passengers on our flight.
   - (A) said
   - (B) told
   - (C) talked
   - (D) mentioned   (   )

3. 11/16 is read as _____.
   - (A) eleven sixteen
   - (B) eleventh sixteen
   - (C) eleven sixteenth
   - (D) eleven sixteenths   (   )

4. We _____ them at football yesterday.
   - (A) won
   - (B) failed
   - (C) beat
   - (D) lost   (   )

5. My friend _____ I supposed would pass the examination has failed.
   - (A) who
   - (B) whom
   - (C) of whom
   - (D) as   (   )

6. _____ in plain English, the book was easy to read.
   - (A) Written
   - (B) Writing
   - (C) To write
   - (D) Having written   ( )

7. Eric and Frank, _____ is my boyfriend, went to the party with me.
   - (A) both of whom
   - (B) either of which
   - (C) either of them
   - (D) neither of whom   ( )

8. At the party, I had my photograph _____ by a friend of mine.
   - (A) take
   - (B) taken
   - (C) to take
   - (D) to be taken   ( )

9. Tom almost never studied while he was at college, _____?
   - (A) didn't he
   - (B) did he
   - (C) wasn't he
   - (D) was he   ( )

10. It's time that Jack _____ a driver's license.
    - (A) gotten
    - (B) got
    - (C) getting
    - (D) to get   ( )

TEST 23 詳解

1.(**C**) He was ***so kind as to*** *give me a ride home.*
他人眞好，開車送我回家。

> ***so ~ as to*** 如此~以致於 (表結果的不定詞片詞)
> ***give sb. a ride*** 開車載某人

2.(**B**) ***All told*** there were some 250 passengers *on our flight.*
我們這班飛機總共有二百五十名乘客。

> ***all told*** 總計 (= *in all* = *in total* = *all together*)
> flight〔flaɪt〕*n.* 班機

3.(**D**) 11/16 is read as <u>eleven sixteenths</u>.
11/16 唸成十六分之十一。

> 1/3 = ***one third***
> 2/3 = ***two thirds*** (分子大於 1，分母須加 s)
> (分數的表示法，詳見文法寶典 p.179)

4.(**C**) We ***beat*** them *at football yesterday.*
我們在昨天的橄欖球賽中打敗了他們。

> 「***beat*** + 對手」，表「打敗」。
> 「***win*** + 比賽、獎品」，表「贏得~比賽、獎品」。(詳見文法寶典 p.301)
> football〔'fʊt,bɔl〕*n.* 橄欖球

5.(**A**) My friend ***who*** *I supposed* ***would pass*** *the examination* has failed.
我以爲會通過考試的那個朋友，結果並沒通過。

> 先行詞是人，空格須做動詞 would pass 的主詞，故關代用主格 who，
> 其後的 I supposed 爲插入語。
> suppose〔sə'poz〕*v.* 以爲

6. (**A**) *Written in plain English*, the book was easy to read.
這本書是用簡易英語寫的，很容易讀。

> 本句是由 *Because the book was written in plain English,…*
> 轉化而來。

7. (**D**) Eric and Frank, **_neither of whom is my boyfriend_**, went to the party with me. (這題常考，因爲關代 whom 未直接放在先行詞後面。)
艾瑞克和法蘭克，兩個都不是我的男朋友，和我一起去參加舞會。

> 空格應填一關代，代替先行詞 Eric and Frank 兩人，引導形容詞子
> 句，故 which 和 them 不合。而 both of them 須接複數動詞 are，
> 在此不合，故選 (D) **_neither of whom_** 表「兩者皆不」。

8. (**B**) *At the party*, I **_had_** my photograph *taken by a friend of mine.* 在宴會中，我請一位朋友替我拍照。

> have 爲使役動詞，其用法爲：
>
> have + 受詞 + $\begin{cases} \text{V. (表主動)} \\ \text{p.p. (表被動)} \end{cases}$ 照片是「被拍攝」，故用過去分詞，選 (B)。。
>
> **_take a photograph_** 拍照

9. (**B**) Tom *almost never* studied *while he was at college,* **_did he_**?
湯姆在大學時代幾乎沒唸什麼書，不是嗎？

> **_did he_**?是 **_did he study_**?的省略。前有否定字 never，故 (A) 不合。

10. (**B**) **_It's time that_** Jack **_got_** *a driver's license.*
是傑克該考駕照的時候了。

> 表「是該～的時候了」，其句型爲：
>
> $\begin{cases} \text{It is time that + S. + 過去式 V. (表與現在事實相反假設)} \\ = \text{It is time that + S. + should + V.} \\ = \text{It is time for + S. + to V.} \end{cases}$

TEST 24

Directions: *Of the four choices given after each sentence, choose the one most suitable for filling in the blank.*

1. He is _____ telling lies.
   - (A) on
   - (B) at
   - (C) from
   - (D) above   ( )

2. If you need reference books, I can lend you _____.
   - (A) it
   - (B) them
   - (C) ones
   - (D) some   ( )

3. Although I am busy, I still _____ some shopping.
   - (A) make
   - (B) do
   - (C) go
   - (D) buy   ( )

4. I don't think it will happen, but if it _____, I won't know what to do.
   - (A) were
   - (B) will
   - (C) had
   - (D) should   ( )

5. Mary, _____ at the sight of the accident, couldn't talk for a while.
   - (A) shocked
   - (B) shocking
   - (C) was shocked
   - (D) having shocked   ( )

6. I think you have the _____ number. This is 2704-5525.

    (A) bad

    (B) different

    (C) strange

    (D) wrong   (   )

7. Don't leave your baggage _____ at any time.

    (A) unattends

    (B) no attend

    (C) unattended

    (D) not attending   (   )

8. He said he would lend me the money if I needed it, and he was as _____ as his word.

    (A) similar

    (B) better

    (C) good

    (D) harsh   (   )

9. Please forgive me _____ to you in a long time.

    (A) not to write

    (B) not for writing

    (C) for not writing

    (D) not to writing   (   )

10. _____ another aspirin if you still have a headache.

    (A) To try to take

    (B) Try to take

    (C) To try taking

    (D) Try taking   (   )

TEST 24 詳解

1. (**D**) He *is above telling* lies.
   他不屑於說謊。

   > *be above* + *V-ing* 不屑於

2. (**D**) *If you need reference books*, I can lend you *some*.
   如果你需要參考書，我可以借你一些。

   > 若指複數名詞，有修飾語時，代名詞用 ones，如 the large ones；
   > 若沒有修飾語時，則用 some，故選 (D)。
   > reference ('rɛfərəns) *n.* 參考

3. (**B**) *Although I am busy*, I *still do some shopping*.
   雖然我很忙，我仍然會去買些東西。

   > *do some shopping* 去購物
   > = *do one's shopping*
   > = *do the shopping*
   > = *go shopping* （不可說成 do shopping）

4. (**D**) I don't think *it will happen, but if it should*, I won't know
   what to do.
   我不認為它會發生，但如果萬一發生了，我不知道該怎麼辦。

   > 助動詞 *should* 作「萬一」解，表可能性極小的假設。

5. (**A**) Mary, *shocked at the sight of the accident*, couldn't talk
   for a while. 瑪麗一看見那場意外，嚇得有好一會兒說不出話來。

   > 本句是由 *Mary, who was shocked at the sight*…，省略關代 who
   > 和 be 動詞 was 簡化而來。shock 是情感動詞，人做主詞，應用過去分詞。
   > shock (ʃɑk) *v.* 使震驚

6. (**D**) I think *you* **have the <u>wrong number</u>**. This is 2704-5525.

我想你打錯電話了。這裏是 2704-5525。

have the wrong number 打錯電話

7. (**C**) Don't **leave** your baggage <u>**unattended**</u> at any time.

任何時候都不要讓你的行李無人看管。

leave 表「任由」，其用法為：

leave + 受詞 + { 形容詞 (表狀態)
V-ing (表主動)
p.p. (表被動)

依句意，選 (C)。

baggage〔'bægɪdʒ〕*n.* 行李
unattended〔ˌʌnə'tɛndɪd〕*adj.* 無人照顧的

8. (**C**) He said *he would lend me the money if I needed it, and* he was **as <u>good</u> as his word.**

他說如果我有需要，他會借錢給我，而他真的信守諾言。

as good as one's word 信守諾言

9. (**C**) Please forgive me *for not writing to you in a long time.*

請原諒我很久都沒寫信給你。

forgive sb. for + V-ing 原諒某人

動名詞的否定，否定的字要放在動名詞前面。

10. (**D**) **<u>*Try taking*</u>** another aspirin *if you still have a headache.*

你如果頭還會痛的話，再吃一顆阿斯匹靈試試看。

依句意為祈使句，須用原形動詞，故 (A)、(C) 不合。

而 { **try + to V.** 設法
try + V-ing 試試看 } 依句意，選 (D)。

吃藥要用 take，不可用 *eat*。　　aspirin〔'æspərɪn〕*n.* 阿斯匹靈

TEST 25

Directions: *Of the four choices given after each sentence, choose the one most suitable for filling in the blank.*

1. My husband has three sisters; they are my _____.
   - (A) sister-in-laws
   - (B) sister-in-law
   - (C) sisters-in-law
   - (D) sisters-in-laws   (   )

2. We have reached the certainty _____ the meeting will be successful.
   - (A) that
   - (B) which
   - (C) if
   - (D) what   (   )

3. The number of students who came up with some answer or other _____ small.
   - (A) was
   - (B) were
   - (C) have been
   - (D) being   (   )

4. I know the author only _____ name.
   - (A) by
   - (B) for
   - (C) of
   - (D) in   (   )

5. I work _____: Monday, Wednesday, and Friday.
   - (A) every day
   - (B) one another day
   - (C) every other day
   - (D) every two other days   (   )

6. _____ from a distance, his house looked like a matchbox.
   (A) Seen
   (B) Seeing
   (C) To see
   (D) Having seen   (   )

7. Not a _____ of the people were suffering from the food poisoning.
   (A) little
   (B) few
   (C) quite
   (D) number   (   )

8. He went to Vienna with a view _____ music.
   (A) of studying
   (B) in studying
   (C) to studying
   (D) to study   (   )

9. She cannot _____ weep at the bad news.
   (A) to
   (B) but
   (C) help
   (D) be to   (   )

10. Two _____ men who saved the child were praised by everyone.
    (A) brave young American
    (B) young brave American
    (C) American young brave
    (D) brave American young   (   )

TEST 25 詳解

1. (**C**) My husband has three sisters; they are my *sisters-in-law*.
   我的丈夫有三個妹妹；她們都是我的小姑。

   > 複合名詞的複數，S 加在主要字之後。如 *sisters-in-law*「大姑；小姑」、
   > *passers-by*「路人」、*shoe-makers*「鞋匠」，*step-mothers*「後母」等。
   > （詳見文法寶典 p.79）

2. (**A**) We have reached the certainty *that* the meeting will be

   successful. 我們確信這場會議會成功。

   > 只有 that 可引導名詞子句，做 certainty 的同位語，that 無代名作用。
   > （詳見文法寶典 p.481）
   > certainty〔ˈsɝtntɪ〕*n.* 確信

3. (**A**) *The number* of students who came up with some answer

   or other was small. 想出某個答案的學生人數很少。

   > 主詞 number（數目）為單數名詞，故動詞須用單數動詞，選 (A)。
   > *come up with* 想出　　*some~or other* 某個

4. (**A**) I *know* the author *only by name*.
   這個作者，我只知道他的名字而已。

   > *know sb. only by name* 只知道某人的名字

5. (**C**) I work *every other day*: *Monday, Wednesday, and Friday*.
   我每隔一天工作：星期一、星期三，及星期五。

   > { *every other day* 每隔一天；每兩天
   > { = *every two days*
   >
   > （注意：「每隔三天」是 every *four* days。）

6. (**A**) *Seen from a distance*, his house looked like a matchbox.
從遠方看來，他的房子就像是個火柴盒。

> 本句是由 *If his house was seen from a distance*, …轉化而來。
> *from a distance* 從遠方　　matchbox〔'mætʃˌbɑks〕*n.* 火柴盒

7. (**B**) *Not a **few*** of the people were suffering from the food poisoning. 那些人當中，有許多人食物中毒。

> $\begin{cases} \textbf{\textit{not a few}} \text{ 很多}（=\textit{many}）[修飾可數名詞]（詳見文法寶典 p.168,170） \\ \textbf{\textit{not a little}} \text{ 很多}（=\textit{much}）[修飾不可數名詞] \end{cases}$
> ***suffer from*** 罹患（病）　　***food poisoning*** 食物中毒

8. (**C**) He went to Vienna *with a view to studying music.*
他去維也納是為了研習音樂。

> 表「目的」的片語：
> $\begin{cases} \textbf{\textit{in order to}} + V. \text{ 為了} \\ = \textbf{\textit{with a view to}} + V\text{-}ing \\ = \textbf{\textit{with an eye to}} + V\text{-}ing \\ = \textbf{\textit{with the purpose of}} + V\text{-}ing \quad \text{Vienna〔vɪ'ɛnə〕} n. \text{ 維也納} \end{cases}$

9. (**B**) She *cannot **but*** weep at the bad news.
聽到那個壞消息，她忍不住哭了起來。

> $\begin{cases} \textbf{\textit{cannot but}} + V. \text{ 忍不住} \\ = \textbf{\textit{cannot help but}} + V. \\ = \textbf{\textit{cannot help}} + V\text{-}ing \quad (\text{help} = \text{avoid}) \end{cases}$
> weep〔wip〕*v.* 哭　　「at＋名詞」表「一聽到；一看到」。

10. (**A**) Two brave young American men *who saved the child* were praised by everyone.
那兩位救了小孩，年輕勇敢的美國人，受到大家的稱讚。

> 形容詞排列的順序為：數量＋性質＋大小＋新舊＋顏色＋國籍＋名詞
> 　　　　　　　　↓　　　↓　　　　　↓　　　　　↓
> （詳見文法寶典 p.190） (Two) (brave)　 (young)　 (American)

TEST 26

Directions: *Of the four choices given after each sentence, choose the one most suitable for filling in the blank.*

1. This car needs _____.
    - (A) to repair
    - (B) repairing
    - (C) having repaired
    - (D) being repaired ( )

2. Mrs. White loves to watch the face of her _____ baby.
    - (A) asleep
    - (B) sleep
    - (C) sleeping
    - (D) slept ( )

3. I don't like cats and my brother doesn't, _____.
    - (A) too
    - (B) also
    - (C) either
    - (D) neither ( )

4. _____ 1100 people live on each square mile of land in that country.
    - (A) Many
    - (B) So many
    - (C) As many as
    - (D) So much as ( )

5. I can't stand _____ any longer.
    - (A) that his nasty attitude
    - (B) his that nasty attitude
    - (C) his nasty attitude of that
    - (D) that nasty attitude of his ( )

6. I would like to make _____ with someone from another country.
   - (A) friend
   - (B) friends
   - (C) a friend
   - (D) friendly   (   )

7. The hospital has two spare beds on the second floor, _____ has been used for years. You are welcome to use either one of them.
   - (A) both of which
   - (B) one of which
   - (C) all of which
   - (D) neither of which   (   )

8. The rumor passed from mouth to mouth _____ he was alive somewhere in the mountains.
   - (A) which
   - (B) what
   - (C) that
   - (D) however   (   )

9. Life changes constantly. Change will always be _____ us.
   - (A) besides
   - (B) doing
   - (C) happening
   - (D) with   (   )

10. In America a number of parents _____ angry and worried about guns easily falling into the hands of their children.
    - (A) is
    - (B) are
    - (C) who is
    - (D) who are   (   )

TEST 26 詳解

1. (**B**) This car *needs repairing*.
   這輛車需要修理。

   > need、want、require 作「需要」解時，接動名詞，只能用主動，
   > 不能用被動的動名詞。needs repairing = needs to be repaired。

2. (**C**) Mrs. White loves to watch the face *of her sleeping baby*.
   懷特太太喜歡看著她的寶寶沉睡中的臉龐。

   > 現在分詞帶有形容詞性質，可修飾名詞表「狀態」，sleeping baby
   > 指「睡著的」寶寶。asleep 亦指「睡著的」，但只能做補語，不可置
   > 於名詞之前。

3. (**C**) I don't like cats and my brother *doesn't, either*.
   我不喜歡貓，我哥哥也不喜歡。

   > 肯定句中的「也」用 too；否定句中的「也」則用 either；*neither* 為
   > 「也不」之意，用於倒裝句，如：I don't like cats and *neither*
   > does my brother.

4. (**C**) *As many as* 1100 people live *on each square mile of land*
   in that country. 該國每平方英哩的土地住著多達一千一百人。

   > *as many as* 接可數名詞，表「多達」，強調數目很大；
   > *as much as* 意義相同，但須接不可數名詞。
   > square (skwɛr) *adj.* 平方的

5. (**D**) I can't stand *that* nasty attitude *of his* any longer.
   我再也無法忍受他討人厭的態度了。

   > 「雙重所有格」的公式為：
   > 「this / that / a(n)… + 名詞 + of + 所有代名詞」(詳見文法寶典 p.108)
   > nasty ('næstɪ) *adj.* 討人厭的

6. (**B**) I would like to ***make friends with*** someone *from another*
country. 我想要和來自其他國家的人交朋友。

  make friends with「與~交朋友」，受詞 friends 一定要用複數。

7. (**D**) The hospital has two spare beds *on the second floor,*
neither of which *has been used for years.* You are
welcome to use either one of them.

  這家醫院二樓有二張備用的床，二張床多年來都未使用。歡迎你使
  用任何一張床。

  關代 which 引導形容詞子句，在子句中 which 代替 two spare
  beds，neither of which 表示「二者皆不」，視為單數；若用
  both of which「二者皆是」則為複數，在此文法不合。

8. (**C**) The rumor passed *from mouth to mouth* *that he was alive*
somewhere in the mountains.
  The rumor 的同位語 ──名詞子句做

  他還活著並住在山區某個地方的謠言，口口相傳地傳開了。

  that 引導 he was…mountains 子句，做 The rumor 的同位語，
  本句為倒裝句。(詳見文法寶典 p.637)

9. (**D**) Life changes *constantly.* Change will *always* be ***with*** us.
  生活不斷地改變。改變總是伴隨著我們。

  介系詞 ***with*** 表「伴隨著；和~一起」。

10. (**B**) *In America* ***a number of*** parents ***are*** angry and worried
about guns *easily falling into the hands of their children.*
  在美國，許多父母很生氣，並擔心槍枝會輕易落入孩子們手中。

  a number of 須接可數複數名詞，表①「幾個」(= *several*)；
  ②「許多」(= *many*)，視前後句意而定。

TEST 27

Directions: *Of the four choices given after each sentence, choose the one most suitable for filling in the blank.*

1. The reason I could not attend the meeting yesterday was _____ I had a severe headache.

    (A) that
    (B) as
    (C) why
    (D) what   ( )

2. _____ if she should know this?

    (A) How
    (B) What
    (C) Which
    (D) Who   ( )

3. The man decided to wait at the station until his wife _____.

    (A) came
    (B) come
    (C) has come
    (D) will come   ( )

4. "Where has she gone?" "How _____ I know?"

    (A) could
    (B) might
    (C) should
    (D) shall   ( )

5. Although he knows nothing about electronics, he speaks _____ an expert.

    (A) like his being
    (B) as if he were
    (C) even if he were
    (D) as though being   ( )

6. The victim is thought _____ a large quantity of poison by mistake.
   - (A) to take
   - (B) to have taken
   - (C) to be taken
   - (D) to have been taken   (   )

7. We didn't _____ to leave Mary out of the plan. It was simply an oversight.
   - (A) forget
   - (B) mean
   - (C) neglect
   - (D) seem   (   )

8. This problem is too simple, so it _____.
   - (A) is hardly worth discussing
   - (B) does hardly worth discussing
   - (C) is hardly worth to discuss
   - (D) does hardly worthy to discuss   (   )

9. He always stays in bed _____ as he can.
   - (A) as lately
   - (B) so lately
   - (C) as late
   - (D) so late   (   )

10. He found five mistakes _____ lines.
   - (A) in as many
   - (B) like so many
   - (C) at so many
   - (D) as many as   (   )

TEST 27 詳解

1.(**A**) ***The reason*** *I could not attend the meeting yesterday **was*** ***that** I had a severe headache.*

我昨天沒有去開會的原因是，我頭痛得很嚴重。

> The reason…is that「…的原因是」，不可說成 *The reason…*
> *is why* 或 *The reason…is because*。
>
> attend〔ə'tɛnd〕*v.* 參加　　severe〔sə'vɪr〕*adj.* 嚴重的

2.(**B**) ***What if*** *she should know this?*

萬一她知道這件事怎麼辦？

> ***What if*~**?「如果~怎麼辦？」是 ***What should we do if*~**? 的省略。

3.(**A**) The man decided to wait *at the station **until** his wife **came**.*

那人決定在車站等到他太太來爲止。

> 主要子句動詞爲過去式時，副詞子句通常爲過去式、過去進行式，或
> 過去完成式，應視句意而定。(詳見文法寶典 p.354)

4.(**C**) "Where has she gone?" "How ***should*** I know?"

「她去哪裏了？」「我怎麼會知道？」

> 疑問句中 ***should*** 表驚訝、不合理、難以相信，或不應該之事。

5.(**B**) *Although he knows nothing about electronics,* he speaks ***as if he were*** *an expert.*

雖然他對電子學一無所知，但他說起話來好像他是專家一樣。

> ***as if*「好像」(= *as though*)，爲連接詞，是假設法，接過去式動
> 詞，表「與現在事實相反」。而 (C) even if「即使」，則不合句意。
> electronics〔ɪˌlɛk'trɑnɪks〕*n.* 電子學

6. (**B**) The victim is thought <u>to have taken</u> a large quantity of poison *by mistake.* 受害者被認為是誤服大量的毒藥。

> 不定詞用「to have + p.p.」表示比主要動詞早發生。be thought 後
> 接不定詞片語，做主詞補語。
>
> victim (ˈvɪktɪm) *n.* 受害者
> ***a large quantity of*** 大量的（接不可數名詞）
> poison (ˈpɔɪzn̩) *n.* 毒藥　　***by mistake*** 錯誤地

7. (**B**) We didn't ***mean to*** leave Mary out of the plan. It was *simply* an oversight.
我們不是故意要把瑪麗從計劃中刪除的。這純粹是一個疏忽。

> ***mean to* + V.** 故意；有意
> ***leave out*** 刪除；遺漏　　oversight (ˌovəˈsaɪt) *n.* 疏忽
> neglect (nɪˈglɛkt) *v.* 疏忽；忽視

8. (**A**) This problem is *too* simple, *so it **is hardly worth discussing**.*
這個問題太容易了，所以幾乎不值得討論。

> worth 是可接受詞的形容詞，「be worth + 動名詞」有三個條件必須
> 遵守：該動名詞必須是主動的，必須是及物動詞，但是不接受詞；
> be worthy 可接 of + N. 或 to V.。

9. (**C**) He *always* stays in bed ***as late* as he can.**
他總是在床上能待多晚就待多晚。

> ***as ~ as one can*** 「儘可能地」（= *as ~ as possible* ）；late 是指時
> 間很晚，而 lately 則為「最近」之意。

10. (**A**) He found five mistakes *in **as many** lines.*
他在五行裏發現了五個錯誤。

> ***as many* = *so many* = *the same number of*** 同樣數目的

TEST 28

Directions: *Of the four choices given after each sentence, choose the one most suitable for filling in the blank.*

1. We shook _____ and parted at the end of our journey.
   - (A) arm
   - (B) arms
   - (C) hands
   - (D) hand ( )

2. It's nice if a child can have _____.
   - (A) a room of himself
   - (B) a room of his own
   - (C) his only room
   - (D) a room of his ( )

3. _____ happens, you may rely on my friendship.
   - (A) Whenever
   - (B) However
   - (C) Whatever
   - (D) Whoever ( )

4. My uncle broke his promise to take us to the beach. _____ my sister was disappointed, her face didn't show it.
   - (A) Even
   - (B) However
   - (C) If
   - (D) Then ( )

5. His clinic _____ many patients since the scandal.
   - (A) loses
   - (B) has lost
   - (C) is losing
   - (D) is lost ( )

6. Extra police _____ to the scene of the trouble.

    (A) was sent
    (B) were sent
    (C) has been sent
    (D) has sent   (   )

7. Mary scarcely seems to care for me, _____?

    (A) does not she
    (B) doesn't she
    (C) does she
    (D) does she not   (   )

8. "What would it cost to _____ this chair repaired?"
"I'd estimate sixty to seventy dollars."

    (A) make
    (B) have
    (C) let
    (D) allow   (   )

9. I never expected that she _____ us.

    (A) joins
    (B) will join
    (C) would join
    (D) has joined   (   )

10. No matter who _____ come, you must not open the
door.

    (A) must
    (B) ought
    (C) may
    (D) are   (   )

TEST 28 詳解

1. (**C**) We *shook hands* and parted *at the end of our journey*.
   在旅程結束時，我們握手道別。

   > *shake hands* 握手（hands 須用複數）　　part〔part〕*v.* 分離
   > journey〔'dʒɜnɪ〕*n.* 旅程

2. (**B**) It's nice *if a child can have* **a room of his own**.
   小孩如果能有自己的房間是很好的。

   > *a room of his own = his own room*
   > *of one's own* 某人自己的

3. (**C**) **Whatever** *happens*, you may rely on my friendship.
   無論發生什麼事，你都可以信任我的友誼。

   > whatever 除引導副詞子句外，在子句中有代名詞的作用，做 happens
   > 的主詞。(A),(B) 無代名詞作用，(D) 不合句意。

4. (**C**) My uncle broke his promise *to take us to the beach*. **If**
   my sister was disappointed, her face didn't show it.
   舅舅說要帶我們去海邊，但他食言了。即使妹妹很失望，她的表情
   並沒有表現出來。

   > if 除了表條件之外，也可表讓步，作「即使」解，等於 even if。
   > *break one's promise* 不守諾言；食言（↔ *keep one's promise*）

5. (**B**) His clinic **has lost** many patients **since the scandal**.
   自從那件醜聞之後，他的診所流失了很多病人。

   > since 要與現在完成式連用，表「從～一直到現在」。
   > clinic〔'klɪnɪk〕*n.* 診所　　scandal〔'skændl〕*n.* 醜聞

6. (**B**) Extra police <u>were sent</u> *to the scene of the trouble.*

更多的警力被派到騷動現場。

extra police = extra policemen。extra police 和 the police 用
法相同,動詞要用複數。若指「一個警察」,要用 a policeman。
extra〔'ɛkstrə〕*adj.* 額外的   scene〔sin〕*n.* 現場

7. (**C**) Mary ***scarcely*** seems to care for me, ***does she***?

瑪麗似乎根本不喜歡我,是嗎?   *care for* 喜歡(用於否定句、疑問句)

scarcely〔'skɛrslɪ〕*adv.* 幾乎不,等於 hardly,句中若有這些字,
即為否定句,故附加問句應用肯定,*does she*? 是 *does she care*
for me? 的省略。碰到任何題目,只要記住,附加問句就是簡單形式
的省略疑問句。

8. (**B**) "What would it cost *to <u>have</u> this chair repaired*?"
"I'd estimate sixty to seventy dollars."

「修理這張椅子要花多少錢?」「我估計大概六、七十元。」

「叫某人做某事」,要用「***have sb. do sth.***」,或「***have sth. done***」。
estimate〔'ɛstə,met〕*v.* 估計

9. (**C**) I *never* expected *that she <u>would join</u> us.*

我從來沒預料到她會加入我們。

expect「預期;預料」後接 that 子句時,子句應是尚未發生之事,
故用未來式,而本句 expected 用過去式,故子句也用未來的過去
式 would。(詳見文法寶典 p.351)

10. (**C**) ***No matter who <u>may</u> come***, you must not open the door.

無論誰來,你都不可以開門。

No matter who 引導副詞子句,表讓步,助動詞應用 may,
但也可不用。故本句可寫成:*No matter who comes, …*。
No matter who 等於 ***Whoever***。

TEST 29

Directions: *Of the four choices given after each sentence, choose the one most suitable for filling in the blank.*

1. They are very proud of _____ students of that college.
   - (A) being
   - (B) to be
   - (C) being not
   - (D) not to be   ( )

2. Let's stop _____ a cup of coffee and take a rest.
   - (A) that have
   - (B) to be having
   - (C) to have
   - (D) having   ( )

3. You must remember _____ him all that you know, when you see him next.
   - (A) telling
   - (B) having told
   - (C) to tell
   - (D) to be told   ( )

4. "Look at this old coin you have here." "It looks rather old, but I don't know whether it's _____ much."
   - (A) excellent
   - (B) worth
   - (C) valuable
   - (D) useful   ( )

5. I'm going to stop her _____ doing that again.
   - (A) ever
   - (B) never
   - (C) once
   - (D) yet   ( )

6. Like _____ stars among the leaves and branches, the street lamps shed their light.
   - (A) very many
   - (B) some many
   - (C) too many
   - (D) so many   (   )

7. They drove to San Francisco taking _____ at the wheel.
   - (A) changes
   - (B) places
   - (C) rides
   - (D) turns   (   )

8. They had games, made good friends, and enjoyed _____ very much.
   - (A) time
   - (B) there
   - (C) them
   - (D) themselves   (   )

9. New York is the city _____ I have long wanted to visit.
   - (A) where
   - (B) which
   - (C) what
   - (D) who   (   )

10. We must admit that there are still many things whose worth cannot be expressed _____ money.
    - (A) in part for
    - (B) in exchange for
    - (C) in favor of
    - (D) in terms of   (   )

TEST 29 詳解

1. (**A**) They are *very* proud of <u>being</u> students *of that college.*
他們非常以身爲那所大學的學生爲傲。

> 介系詞之後要接名詞或動名詞做受詞。

2. (**C**) Let's *stop **to have*** a cup of coffee ***and*** take a rest.
讓我們停下來喝杯咖啡，休息一下。

> $\begin{cases} \textit{stop} + \textit{\textbf{to}} \ \textit{V.} \ \text{停下來，去做某事} \\ \textit{stop} + \textit{\textbf{V-ing}} \ \text{停止做某事} \end{cases}$

3. (**C**) You must *remember **to tell*** him all *that you know, when you see him next.*
你下次看到他時，要記得告訴他你所知道的一切。

> $\begin{cases} \textit{remember} + \textit{to} \ \textit{V.} \ \text{記得要去做某事（還沒做）} \\ \textit{remember} + \textit{V-ing} \ \text{記得做過某事（已經做了）} \end{cases}$

4. (**B**) "Look at this old coin *you have here.*" "It looks *rather*

   old, but I don't know *whether it's <u>worth</u> much.*"
「看看你這裏的這個舊硬幣。」
「看起來是相當舊，但不知道是不是很值錢。」

> much 在此爲代名詞，代替 much money；worth 爲特殊形容詞，可
> 接受詞，但不置於名詞之前，worth 後與名詞、代名詞及動名詞連用。

5. (**A**) I'm going to stop her <u>*ever*</u> doing that *again.*
我將要阻止她絕不可再做那件事了。

> ever 在此純粹用來加強語氣，等於 at any time。

6. (**D**) Like ___so many___ *stars among the leaves and branches*, the street lamps shed their light.
街燈散發出燈光，就像那麼多的星星躲在枝葉間。

    so many = ***the same number of*** 同樣數目的
    branch〔bræntʃ〕*n.* 樹枝　　shed〔ʃɛd〕*v.* 散發（光、熱、味道）

7. (**D**) They drove to San Francisco *taking turns at the wheel*.
他們輪流開車到舊金山。

    take turns 輪流　　wheel〔hwil〕*n.* 方向盤（=*steering wheel*）
    at the wheel 開車

8. (**D**) They had games, made good friends, and *enjoyed* ___themselves___ *very much*.
他們玩遊戲、交到好朋友，玩得非常愉快。

    enjoy oneself 玩得愉快（=*have fun* = *have a good time*）

9. (**B**) New York is the city ___which___ *I have long wanted to visit*.
紐約是我長久以來一直想要造訪的都市。

    關代 which 引導形容詞子句，在子句中 which 做 visit 的受詞。
    (A) 是關係副詞，無代名詞作用。（詳見文法寶典 p.243）

10. (**D**) We must admit *that there are still many things* whose *worth cannot be expressed* ___in terms of___ *money*.
我們必須承認，仍然有很多事物的價值不能以金錢的觀點來表達。

    in exchange for 交換　　***in favor of*** 贊成；支持
    in terms of 以~觀點

TEST 30

Directions: *Of the four choices given after each sentence, choose the one most suitable for filling in the blank.*

1. Today's high temperature set a new record. It's extremely hot _____ this time of the year.

   (A) for
   (B) on
   (C) in
   (D) about   (   )

2. _____ grazing in the field.

   (A) A cattle was
   (B) A herd of cattles was
   (C) Cattle were
   (D) Cattles were   (   )

3. The Government ordered that the price of household soap _____ reduced by two pence.

   (A) be
   (B) is
   (C) had been
   (D) can be   (   )

4. This is the best book that I have _____ read.

   (A) once
   (B) ever
   (C) never
   (D) still   (   )

5. You had better _____ your hair cut.

   (A) had
   (B) have
   (C) to get
   (D) to have   (   )

6. He spoke _____ he knew all about our plans when in fact he knew nothing about them.
   - (A) that
   - (B) as though
   - (C) even though
   - (D) although   (   )

7. John and Mary _____ meet us at the airport.
   - (A) are have to
   - (B) are to
   - (C) will to
   - (D) will be going to   (   )

8. Have you ever tried _____ on the river?
   - (A) skate
   - (B) skating
   - (C) to be skating
   - (D) to have skated   (   )

9. She is rather _____ at tennis.
   - (A) short
   - (B) low
   - (C) small
   - (D) poor   (   )

10. The money will be divided _____ between the two of them.
    - (A) evenly
    - (B) sharply
    - (C) flatly
    - (D) commonly   (   )

TEST 30 詳解

1. (**A**) Today's high temperature set a new record. It's *extremely*
   hot **_for_** *this time of the year.*
   今天的高溫創下新記錄。對於一年中的這個時間而言，今天非常熱。

   介系詞 *for* 可表「對～而言；就～而論」，相當於 considering 或
   in view of。
   record (ˈrɛkəd) *n.* 記錄　　***set a record*** 創記錄

2. (**C**) <u>Cattle were</u> grazing *in the field.* 牛在原野上吃草。

   cattle (ˈkætḷ) *n.* 牛，和 mankind（人類）一樣，是單數形式不加 s，
   但作複數，須接複數動詞。
   graze (grez) *v.* 吃草　　herd (hɜd) *n.* (牛) 群

3. (**A**) The Government ***ordered that*** the price of household soap

   _be_ reduced *by two pence.*
   政府下令，家庭用肥皂的價格應該要降二分。

   order 為慾望動詞，接 that 子句時，子句中的動詞應用「should+V.」，
   而 should 可省略。
   household (ˈhaʊsˌhold) *adj.* 家庭的　　soap (sop) *n.* 肥皂

4. (**B**) This is the best book *that I have **_ever_** read.*
   這是我所讀過最好的書。

   ever 可用來加強最高級的語氣，等於 at any time。本句中文也
   可翻成「我從來沒讀過這麼好的書。」，但英文不可用 *never*。

5. (**B**) You ***had better*** <u>have</u> your hair cut.
   你最好去剪頭髮。

   had better「最好」，後面要接原形動詞。

6. (**B**) He spoke ***as though*** *he knew all about our plans when in fact he knew nothing about them.*

   他說起話來好像他知道我們所有的計劃，但事實上他一無所知。

   as though 好像；彷彿 (= *as if*)
   even though 即使 (= *even if*)

7. (**B**) John and Mary ***are to meet*** *us at the airport.*

   約翰和瑪麗會來機場接我們。

   「***be to + V.***」，表「預定」。
   meet〔mit〕*v.* 接

8. (**B**) Have you *ever **tried** **skating** on the river?*

   你試過在河面上溜冰嗎？

   { ***try + V-ing*** 試試看
   { ***try + to V.*** 努力去做
   skate〔sket〕*v.* 溜冰

9. (**D**) She ***is** rather **poor** at tennis.*

   她的網球打得很爛。

   be poor at 「不擅長；很笨拙」，相反用法為 be good at 「擅長」。

10. (**A**) The money will be divided *evenly between the two of them.* 這筆錢將會被他們二人平分。

    本題考句意。
    evenly〔'ivənlɪ〕*adv.* 平均地；平等地
    sharply〔'ʃɑrplɪ〕*adv.* 銳利地；急速地
    flatly〔'flætlɪ〕*adv.* 平坦地；單調地

TEST 31

Directions: *Of the four choices given after each sentence, choose the one most suitable for filling in the blank.*

1. Sunlight is no _____ necessary to good health than fresh air.
   - (A) more
   - (B) better
   - (C) further
   - (D) less   (　)

2. After a hard argument we weren't on speaking _____.
   - (A) moods
   - (B) connections
   - (C) terms
   - (D) circles   (　)

3. He was patience _____.
   - (A) all
   - (B) at all
   - (C) itself
   - (D) himself   (　)

4. This is the reason for _____ he did it.
   - (A) why
   - (B) what
   - (C) which
   - (D) that   (　)

5. You won't be able to reach the airport in time _____ you drive faster.
   - (A) unless
   - (B) if
   - (C) even
   - (D) if not   (　)

6. What is the weather in your hometown _____ about this
time of the year?

   (A) likely
   (B) like
   (C) liked
   (D) alike   (   )

7. He is the man _____ I believe can help you.

   (A) as
   (B) who
   (C) whom
   (D) whomever   (   )

8. _____ is no telling how long their quarrel will last.

   (A) He
   (B) One
   (C) There
   (D) This   (   )

9. We _____ attend the meeting.

   (A) had no better
   (B) had better not
   (C) not had better
   (D) had not better to   (   )

10. Look! What a beautiful house! How I wish I _____
a house like that.

   (A) could buy
   (B) can buy
   (C) have bought
   (D) can have bought   (   )

TEST 31 詳解

1. (**D**) Sunlight is *no less* necessary *to good health* **than** *fresh air.*
   陽光與新鮮空氣對健康一樣必要。

   > *no less ~ than* 和…一樣 (= *as ~ as*)
   > *no more ~ than* 和…一樣不 (= *not ~ any more than*)

   no less ~ than 的記法很容易，no 在此是副詞，等於 not at all，字面意思是「一點也不少於」，引申為「和…一樣」。(詳見文法寶典 p.202)

2. (**C**) *After a hard argument* we weren't on speaking <u>terms</u>.
   大吵一架後，我們就不說話了。

   terms 指「條件、關係、措詞」等意時，均用複數形。
   be on good terms with sb. 與某人友善、關係好
   be not on speaking terms with sb. 不願與某人交談
   argument ('argjəmənt) *n.* 爭吵

3. (**C**) He was patience *itself*.
   他非常有耐心。

   > 抽象名詞 + itself
   > = all + 抽象名詞
   > = very + 形容詞

   > patience itself
   > = all patience
   > = very patient

4. (**C**) This is the reason *for **which*** he did it.
   這就是他為何做此事的原因。

   形容詞子句中用 which 代替先行詞 reason，for which = why。

5. (**A**) You won't be able to reach the airport *in time **unless***
   you drive faster.
   除非你開快一點，否則你無法及時到達機場。

   unless「除非」，相當於 if…not…「如果不…」。

6. (**B**) What is the weather *in your hometown* <u>like</u> *about this time of the year*? 在一年的這個時候，你的故鄉天氣如何？

　　疑問詞 what 做介系詞 like 的受詞；what is ~ like = how is ~。
　　hometown〔'hom,taʊn〕*n.* 故鄉

7. (**B**) He is the man <u>who</u> I believe can help you.
他就是我相信能幫你的人。

　　形容詞子句中，缺乏主詞，故關代應用 who。I believe 爲插入語，
　　並不影響子句的結構。插入語的動詞通常是 think、believe、guess、
　　imagine。

8. (**C**) ***There is no telling*** how long their quarrel will last.
我們無法得知他們的爭執會持續多久。

　　There is no + V-ing 不可能 (= *It is impossible to + V.*)
　　quarrel〔'kwɔrəl〕*n.* 爭吵　　last〔læst〕*v.* 持續

9. (**B**) We ***had better not*** attend the meeting.
我們最好別去參加會議。

　　had better 的否定是 ***had better not*** 或 ***hadn't better***，不可寫
　　成 ***had not better***。
　　attend〔ə'tɛnd〕*v.* 參加

10. (**A**) Look! What a beautiful house! ***How I wish I <u>could buy</u>*** a house like that.
你看！那棟房子好漂亮！要是我能買一棟像那樣的房子不知該有多好。

　　How I wish …「要是…不知該有多好」，表與事實不符或不可能實現
　　的強烈願望，後面應用假設法動詞。(詳見文法寶典 p.370)

TEST 32

Directions: *Of the four choices given after each sentence, choose the one most suitable for filling in the blank.*

1. You are _____ here by midnight, or you'll get punished.
   - (A) return
   - (B) being returned
   - (C) returned
   - (D) to return   ( )

2. His mother has been _____ a drugstore for fifteen years.
   - (A) running
   - (B) having
   - (C) taking
   - (D) making   ( )

3. We had to drive very slowly _____ fog.
   - (A) instead of
   - (B) according to
   - (C) by means of
   - (D) on account of   ( )

4. His work is _____ satisfactory and therefore, he has been asked to do it over again.
   - (A) far from
   - (B) a little bit
   - (C) very much
   - (D) extremely   ( )

5. I've already had one bad experience buying goods by mail order and I don't want _____.
   - (A) another
   - (B) any longer
   - (C) at all
   - (D) other   ( )

6. The boy took great _____ to try to work out the problem.
   - (A) effects
   - (B) struggles
   - (C) senses
   - (D) pains   (   )

7. She went _____ to say that he was a swindler.
   - (A) too far
   - (B) so far as
   - (C) so long as
   - (D) too long   (   )

8. The bomb fell within about twenty paces of _____ we had been sitting.
   - (A) which
   - (B) the place of
   - (C) what
   - (D) where   (   )

9. This dish looks terrible! I wouldn't eat it _____ I were starving.
   - (A) after
   - (B) because
   - (C) even if
   - (D) only when   (   )

10. If people become sleepy when they read good books, it is _____ they are unwilling to make the effort, _____ they do not know how to make it.
    - (A) not because ; but because
    - (B) not as ; but as
    - (C) either ; or
    - (D) neither ; nor   (   )

TEST 32 詳解

1. (**D**) You *are to return* here *by midnight,* or you'll get punished.
   你必須在午夜之前回到這裏,否則你會受到處罰。

   「*be + to V.*」可表「義務」,作「應該;必須」解。

2. (**A**) His mother *has been running* a drugstore *for fifteen years.*
   他的母親經營一家藥房已經十五年了。

   run 在此作「經營」解,是及物動詞。而表「從過去一直到現在,並強調動作仍在持續」,須用「現在完成進行式」。

3. (**D**) We had to drive *very slowly* *on account of* fog.
   由於有霧,我們必須開得很慢。

   on account of「由於」(= *because of* = *as a result of* = *owing to* = *due to*) 為介系詞的片語,又稱為「片語介系詞」,後接名詞做受詞。
   instead of 而不是　　*by means of* 藉由

4. (**A**) His work is *far from* satisfactory and *therefore,* he has
   been asked to do it *over again.*
   他的工作一點也不令人滿意,因此他被要求再重做一次。

   far from 一點也不 (= *not~at all* = *not~in the least*)
   satisfactory 〔‚sætɪsˈfæktərɪ 〕*adj.* 令人滿意的

5. (**A**) I've *already* had *one* bad experience *buying goods by mail*
   order and I don't want *another.*
   我已經有一次郵購買東西不愉快的經驗了,我不想再有第二次。

   不指定時,one 和 another 連用,another 為代名詞,在此指
   another bad experience。(詳見文法寶典 p.141)

   $\begin{cases} \textit{one···another} & \text{一個···另一個} \\ \textit{some···others} & \text{一些···另一些} \end{cases}$

6. (**D**) The boy *took* great *pains* to try to work out the problem.
這個男孩非常努力，試著解決這個問題。

> *take pains*「非常努力」，pains 作「努力」解，為複數形，但有
> 一個例外：No pain(s), no gain(s). (不勞則無穫。)
> *work out* 解決　　effect〔ɪ'fɛkt〕*n.* 影響；效果
> struggle〔'strʌgl〕*n.* 掙扎；奮鬥

7. (**B**) She *went so far as to* say *that he was a swindler.*
她竟然說他是個騙子。

> *go so far as to* + *V.* 竟然；甚至　　*so far as* 到達～程度
> swindler〔'swɪndlɚ〕*n.* 騙子

8. (**D**) The bomb fell *within about twenty paces of **where** we had
been sitting.* 炸彈掉在我們之前坐的地方大約二十步距離之內。

> 本句原為…*paces of the place where we had*…，先行詞為
> the place 時，可省略。
> bomb〔bɑm〕*n.* 炸彈　　pace〔pes〕*n.* 一步

9. (**C**) This dish looks terrible! I wouldn't eat it *even if I were
starving.* 這道菜看起來真可怕！即使餓死了，我也不吃。

> *even if*「即使」後可接直說法和假設法，本句因有 *I were*，可知
> 為假設法，其他答案均須接直說法。
> dish〔dɪʃ〕*n.* 一道菜　　starve〔stɑrv〕*v.* 飢餓

10. (**A**) *If people become sleepy when they read good books,* it is
not because they are unwilling to make the effort, *but
because* they do not know *how* to make it.
如果人們閱讀好書會想睡覺，不是因為他們不願努力，而是因為他
們不知如何努力。

> 「*not~but*…」表「不是～，而是…」，可以連接二個 because 子句，
> 但不可接二個 as 子句。
> unwilling〔ʌn'wɪlɪŋ〕*adj.* 不願意的

TEST 33

Directions: *Of the four choices given after each sentence, choose the one most suitable for filling in the blank.*

1. _____ white, this house looks bigger.
   - (A) Paint
   - (B) Painting
   - (C) Painted
   - (D) To paint   (   )

2. He couldn't get the car _____ and went by bus.
   - (A) start
   - (B) to start
   - (C) starting
   - (D) be started   (   )

3. The students played _____ on April Fools' Day.
   - (A) to their teacher a trick
   - (B) their teacher a trick
   - (C) their teacher at a trick
   - (D) their teacher by a trick   (   )

4. No matter what you _____ me to do, I'll do it.
   - (A) hope
   - (B) have
   - (C) wish
   - (D) make   (   )

5. The American consumer is more and more interested in food that has no artificial ingredients _____ to it.
   - (A) added
   - (B) adding
   - (C) having added
   - (D) to add   (   )

6. David is an honest boy. His honest deed is _____ praised.

   (A) worth
   (B) worth of
   (C) worthy to be
   (D) worthy of   ( )

7. Richard studied so hard _____ well on the test.

   (A) that he had not done
   (B) that he should not have done
   (C) that he must have done
   (D) that he had to be done   ( )

8. The play was a lot of fun. I wish you _____ there.

   (A) could be
   (B) could have been
   (C) have been
   (D) would be   ( )

9. You only started this job an hour ago; surely you _____ it, have you?

   (A) finished
   (B) have finished
   (C) haven't been finished
   (D) haven't finished   ( )

10. The English of this composition is too good. She can't _____ it herself.

   (A) have to write
   (B) have written
   (C) had written
   (D) be written   ( )

TEST 33 詳解

1. (**C**) *Painted* white, this house looks bigger.
因為漆成白色，所以這間房子看起來比較大。

> 本句是由 *Because it is painted* <u>*white*</u> 轉化而來的分詞構句。
> 　　　　　　　　　　　　主詞補語

2. (**B**) He couldn't *get the car to start* and went by bus.
他無法發動車子，所以搭公車去。

> 動詞 get 可表「使」之意，含意和使役動詞相同，但它不是使役
> 動詞，故受詞補語還是須用帶 to 的不定詞。

3. (**B**) The students *played* their teacher *a trick* on April Fools' Day.
這些學生在愚人節對老師惡作劇。

> play 表「開玩笑；惡作劇」之意時，為授與動詞，可直接接二個受詞。
> *play sb. a trick* = *play a trick on sb.*

4. (**C**) *No matter what you* <u>***wish***</u> *me to do*, I'll do it.
無論你希望我去做什麼，我都會去做。

> wish 接受詞後，可接不定詞做受詞補語，have 和 make 為使役動
> 詞，應用原形動詞做受詞補語，而 hope 則無此用法。

5. (**A**) The American consumer is more and more interested in
food *that has no artificial ingredients* ***added*** *to it.*
美國消費者對於沒有添加人工成分的食物，越來越感興趣。

> 依句意，人工成分被加入食物中，為被動，故用過去分詞 *added*。
> consumer (kən'sumɚ) *n.* 消費者
> artificial (ˌɑrtə'fɪʃəl) *adj.* 人工的；人造的
> ingredient (ɪn'gridɪənt) *n.* 成分；材料

6. (**C**) David is an honest boy. His honest deed is ___worthy to be___
___praised___. 大衛是個誠實的孩子。他誠實的行為值得被稱讚。

> 表「值得稱讚」，可用「*be worthy of praise*」，或「*be worthy to be praised*」，也可用「*be worth praising*」。
>
> deed〔did〕*n.* 行為　　praise〔prez〕*v., n.* 稱讚

7. (**C**) Richard studied *so hard that he must have done* well
on the test. 理查如此用功讀書，他考試一定考得很好。

> { *must* + *V.* 表「對現在肯定事實的推測」。
> { *must have* + *p.p.* 則表「對過去肯定事實的推測」。

8. (**B**) The play was a lot of fun. I *wish you could have been*
there. 比賽好有趣，我真希望你當時也能在場。

> wish 之後，表「與過去事實相反的假設」，要用「had + p.p.」或「would / could / should / might + have + p.p.」。(詳見文法寶典 p.369)

9. (**D**) You *only* started this job *an hour ago*; *surely* you haven't
finished it, *have you*?
你一小時前才開始做這個工作；當然你還沒做完，是嗎？

> 附加問句 have you 是 have you finished it 的省略，可知前面為現在完成式，且為否定。

10. (**B**) The English *of this composition* is *too* good. She *can't*
___have written___ it *herself*.
這篇作文的英文太好了。不可能是她自己寫的。

> { *can't* + *V.* 表「對現在或未來否定的推測」。
> { *can't have* + *p.p.* 表「對過去否定的推測」。
> composition〔ˌkɑmpəˈzɪʃən〕*n.* 作文

TEST 34

Directions: *Of the four choices given after each sentence, choose the one most suitable for filling in the blank.*

1. How lonely and helpless she must feel left all _____!
   - (A) over the world
   - (B) the more
   - (C) work and no play
   - (D) by herself   ( )

2. Pat is very talkative. This is _____ I don't like him.
   - (A) what
   - (B) why
   - (C) that
   - (D) because   ( )

3. Let's get going in case the bus _____ early.
   - (A) doesn't leave
   - (B) leaves
   - (C) will leave
   - (D) won't leave   ( )

4. On such a hot day, I prefer _____ at home _____ out.
   - (A) stay ; to go
   - (B) staying ; to going
   - (C) to stay ; than to go
   - (D) staying ; than going   ( )

5. It struck me as strange _____ my front door was open when I got home.
   - (A) which
   - (B) as
   - (C) what
   - (D) that   ( )

6. I _____ to Italy, though I've always wanted to go.
   - (A) have been
   - (B) have never been
   - (C) had never gone
   - (D) had gone   (   )

7. She was _____ than angry when her son lied again.
   - (A) sader
   - (B) sadder
   - (C) more sad
   - (D) much sad   (   )

8. A famous cellist _____ from Germany will give a recital tonight.
   - (A) returned
   - (B) returning
   - (C) being returned
   - (D) having returning   (   )

9. Do you know that Japan once produced more silk than _____ country?
   - (A) different
   - (B) other
   - (C) another
   - (D) any other   (   )

10. He was one of the famous men of _____ of his time.
    - (A) book
    - (B) writings
    - (C) letters
    - (D) papers   (   )

TEST 34 詳解

1. (**D**) How lonely and helpless she must feel *left all **by herself***!
被獨自留下來，她一定覺得很寂寞無助吧！

> 後半句為 *when she is left*⋯省略而來的分詞構句。
> ***by oneself***「獨自」(= *alone*)，all 為加強語氣用法，也可省略，
> 其他答案皆不合句意。

2. (**B**) Pat is *very* talkative. This is ***why** I don't like him.*
派特非常愛講話，這就是我不喜歡他的原因。

> why 引導表原因的形容詞子句中，先行詞 the reason 可省略；
> 亦可把 why⋯him 視為一個名詞子句，做主詞補語。

3. (**B**) Let's get going *in case the bus **leaves** early.*
我們走吧，以免公車提早出發。

> 「*in case (that)* + 子句」，表「以免；以防萬一」，子句中可用
> 助動詞 should，也可用直說法動詞。(詳見文法寶典 p.514)

4. (**B**) *On such a hot day,* I ***prefer** staying at home **to** going* out.
在這樣的大熱天，我寧願待在家裏也不要出門。

> ***prefer** + V-ing + to + V-ing* 寧願⋯也不願
> (= *prefer to + V. + rather than + V.*)

5. (**D**) It struck me as strange ***that** my front door was open when*

I got home. 我覺得很奇怪，當我回到家時，我的前門是開著的。

> It 是虛主詞，that 引導 my front⋯got home，才是真正主詞。
> ***sth. strike sb. as*** 某人覺得某事

6. (**B**) I have *never* been to Italy, *though I've always wanted to go.*

我從未去過義大利，雖然我一直很想去。

> 現在完成式可表從過去到現在的經驗；*have been to* 指「曾經去過」；*have gone to* 指「已經到」。

7. (**C**) She was ***more*** sad ***than*** angry *when her son lied again.*

當她的兒子再度說謊時，與其說她生氣，不如說她傷心。

> 「*more~than…*」指同一個人二種不同特性的比較時，解釋為「與其說…，不如說~」，原來比較級字尾加 er 的形容詞，一律用「more~than…」，不加 er。

8. (**B**) A famous cellist *returning from Germany* will give a recital *tonight.*

從德國回來的一位名大提琴家，今晚將舉行獨奏會。

> 本句原為…*cellist who returned from*…省略關代 who，改為分詞片語 returning…。
>
> cellist ('tʃɛlɪst) *n.* 大提琴家　　recital (rɪ'saɪtl) *n.* 獨奏會

9. (**D**) Do you know *that Japan once produced more silk than* ***any other*** *country?*

你知道日本曾經生產比其他任何國家都要多的絲嗎？

> 用比較級表最高級，一定要用 any other…，自己不得包含在內，不可只用 any。

10. (**C**) He was one of the famous ***men of letters*** *of his time.*

他是當代最有名的作家之一。

> ***a man of letters***「文學家；作家」，複數形 letters 作「文學」解。

TEST 35

Directions: *Of the four choices given after each sentence, choose the one most suitable for filling in the blank.*

1. He will return the book as soon as he _____ with it.

   (A) will do
   (B) has done
   (C) will have done
   (D) will be done   (   )

2. The river is very dangerous _____.

   (A) to swim
   (B) swim
   (C) to swim in
   (D) swim in   (   )

3. _____ more pleasant than traveling.

   (A) Nothing is
   (B) Another thing is not
   (C) Anything is not
   (D) Not at all   (   )

4. _____ I admit that the problem is difficult, I still believe it is solvable.

   (A) If
   (B) While
   (C) Because
   (D) Despite   (   )

5. Dark _____ it was, we managed to find our way home.

   (A) after
   (B) although
   (C) as
   (D) before   (   )

6. A large proportion of _____ English-speaking people watch on TV is of American origin.

   (A) that
   (B) what
   (C) where
   (D) which   (   )

7. As I was invited to the party, I was _____ myself with pleasure.

   (A) at
   (B) beside
   (C) for
   (D) over   (   )

8. Water turns _____ ice at 32 °F.

   (A) off
   (B) out
   (C) up
   (D) into   (   )

9. It was a terrifying experience to _____ the world rocking during the earthquake.

   (A) feel
   (B) fall
   (C) fell
   (D) felt   (   )

10. I've never heard you are in this town. How long _____?

    (A) are you here
    (B) had you been here
    (C) were you here
    (D) have you been here   (   )

TEST 35 詳解

1.(**B**) He will return the book *as soon as he __has done__ with it.*
一等他看完那本書,他就會歸還它。

> 表時間的副詞子句中,不能以 shall、will 表示未來,要用現在式代替
> 未來式,現在完成式代替未來完成式。
>
> *__have done with__* 完成;結束

2.(**C**) The river is *very* dangerous *__to swim in__*.
在這條河裏游泳非常危險。

> 被不定詞所修飾的名詞或代名詞,就是不定詞意義上的受詞,不可寫
> 成 *to swim* 或 *to swim in it*。

3.(**A**) *__Nothing__ is __more__ pleasant __than traveling__*.
沒有一件事比旅行更愉快。

> 「*__Nothing is__* + 比較級 + *__than__*」表「沒有一件事比~更」,相當於最
> 高級之意。

4.(**B**) *__While__ I admit that the problem is difficult*, I *still* believe
it is solvable.
雖然我承認這個問題很困難,但我仍相信它是可以解決的。

> while 可引導表讓步的副詞子句,作「雖然」解。(詳見文法寶典 p.528)
> solvable〔'sɑlvəbḷ〕*adj.* 可以解決的

5.(**C**) *Dark __as__ it was*, we managed to find our way home.
雖然天色很暗,我們還是設法找到回家的路。

> as 作「雖然」解,用於倒裝句,也可用 though 代換,句型為:
> 「形容詞/不加冠詞的名詞 + as/though + 主詞 + 動詞」。
> 本句相當於:Although/Though it was dark…。

6. (**B**) A large proportion of _**what**_ *English-speaking people watch*
on TV is of American origin.

說英語的人在電視上所看的，大部分都源自美國。

複合關代 what，引導名詞子句，做介系詞 of 的受詞，在子句中，
what 做 watch 的受詞，此時 what = the thing that，因為 what
代表二個以上的字，所以稱為複合關係代名詞。

proportion〔prə'porʃən〕*n.* 比例
origin〔'ɔrədʒɪn〕*n.* 起源

7. (**B**) *As I was invited to the party*, I was _**beside**_ **myself with**
pleasure.　當我受邀參加宴會時，我真是欣喜若狂。

**be beside oneself with** 因~而忘形、發狂

8. (**D**) Water _**turns**_ _**into**_ ice *at 32 °F.*

水在華氏 32 度會變成冰。

**turn into** 變成

9. (**A**) It was a terrifying experience to _**feel**_ the world _**rocking**_

during the earthquake.

在地震中，感覺整個世界都在搖晃，真是個嚇人的經驗。

feel 為感官動詞，可接原形動詞或分詞做受詞補語；
fall「落下」，fell「砍伐」，均不合句意，也無此用法。
terrifying〔'tɛrə,faɪɪŋ〕*adj.* 嚇人的
rock〔rɑk〕*v.* 搖

10. (**D**) I've _**never**_ heard *you are in this town.* How long have
you been here?

我從來沒聽說你在鎮上。你在這兒待多久了？

表「從過去某個時間持續到現在」，應用現在完成式。

TEST 36

Directions: *Of the four choices given after each sentence, choose the one most suitable for filling in the blank.*

1. She has not come here yet. I am afraid she _____ her way.
   - (A) may be lost
   - (B) may have lost
   - (C) may be having lost
   - (D) may have been lost   ( )

2. If _____ I could speak English as fluently as you!
   - (A) not
   - (B) so be
   - (C) only
   - (D) merely   ( )

3. She is very frugal, not to _____ stingy.
   - (A) remark
   - (B) say
   - (C) speak
   - (D) tell   ( )

4. A serious illness _____ him to drop out of school.
   - (A) made
   - (B) let
   - (C) had
   - (D) caused   ( )

5. It was very sensible _____ him to reject the bribe.
   - (A) to
   - (B) of
   - (C) with
   - (D) about   ( )

6. _____ beautiful roses you sent me! It was nice of you.

    (A) How
    (B) What
    (C) Which
    (D) That   (   )

7. At _____ time in my life have I been busier than I am today.

    (A) any
    (B) no
    (C) other
    (D) some   (   )

8. Next to my house lives a _____ teacher.

    (A) retire
    (B) retiring
    (C) retired
    (D) retirement   (   )

9. I burst out laughing _____ myself.

    (A) regardless of
    (B) in spite of
    (C) forgetting about
    (D) against   (   )

10. He said he couldn't speak Russian, _____ was untrue.

    (A) which
    (B) what
    (C) why
    (D) how   (   )

TEST 36 詳解

1.(**B**) She has not come *here yet*. I am afraid *she **may have lost** her way*. 她還沒到這裏，恐怕她迷路了。

> *may + V.* 表「對現在或未來的推測」。
> *may have + p.p.* 表「對過去的推測」。

2.(**C**) *If **only** I could speak English as fluently as you!*
要是我的英文能說得和你--樣流利就好了！

> *If only* 和 *I wish* 一樣，表「不可能實現的願望」，接過去式子句，表「與現在事實相反」，接過去完成式子句，則表「與過去事實相反」。

3.(**B**) She is *very* frugal, *not to **say*** stingy.
她雖然不能說吝嗇，但也非常節儉。

> *not to say*「雖然不能說」，和 to say nothing of「更別提」，均是「獨立不定詞片語」，但句意不同，不可混用。所謂「獨立不定詞片語」，即和主要子句的文法無關聯。
>
> frugal〔'frugl〕*adj.* 節儉的　　stingy〔'stɪndʒɪ〕*adj.* 吝嗇的

4.(**D**) A serious illness ***caused him to drop*** out of school.
一場重病使他輟學。

> cause 和 get，意義上像使役動詞，但後面都要接帶 to 的不定詞，做受詞補語。make、let、have 均為使役動詞，接受詞後應接原形動詞。

5.(**B**) *It was very **sensible of him*** to reject the bribe.
他拒絕收受賄賂是非常明智的。

> 形容詞修飾後面的人，表對此人的稱讚或批評時，介系詞用 *of*，和 *It's kind of you*…用法相同。
>
> sensible〔'sɛnsəbḷ〕*adj.* 明智的　　bribe〔braɪb〕*n.* 賄賂

6. (**B**) ***What*** beautiful roses you sent me! It was nice of you.
　　　你送我的玫瑰花好漂亮喔！你眞好！

> 感歎句的句型爲：　⎧ How + 形容詞或副詞 + 主詞 + 動詞！
> （詳見文法寶典 p.4）　⎨ How + 形容詞 + a(n) + 單數名詞 + 主詞 + 動詞！
> 　　　　　　　　　　⎨ What + a(n) + (形容詞) + 單數名詞 + 主詞 + 動詞！
> 　　　　　　　　　　⎩ What + 形容詞 + 複數名詞 + 主詞 + 動詞！

7. (**B**) ***At no time in my life*** have I been busier ***than*** *I am today*.
　　　在我的生命中，沒有一段時間比我現在更忙。

> 否定副詞置於句首，助動詞 have 和主詞 I 要倒裝。

8. (**C**) ‾Next to my house‾ lives a <u>retired</u> teacher.
　　　我家隔壁住了一位已退休的老師。

> 不及物動詞的過去分詞不表「被動」，而表「主動、完成」之意。
> 本句爲倒裝句，主詞是 a retired teacher。（詳見文法寶典 p.631）

9. (**B**) I burst out laughing ***in spite of myself***.
　　　我不由自主地放聲大笑。

> ***in spite of oneself*** 不由自主地；情不自禁地
> ***burst out + V-ing*** 突然
> ***regardless of*** 無論

10. (**A**) He said *he couldn't speak Russian*, ───先行詞─── ───形容詞子句───
which *was untrue*.
　　　他說他不會說俄文，這不是眞的。

> 關代 which 引導形容詞子句，修飾先行詞 he couldn't speak
> Russian，在形容詞子句中，which 代替先行詞，做 was 的主詞。
> Russian〔'rʌʃən〕*n.* 俄文

TEST 37

Directions: *Of the four choices given after each sentence, choose the one most suitable for filling in the blank.*

1. She was able to go to college _____ the scholarship.
   - (A) to
   - (B) in
   - (C) according to
   - (D) thanks to   ( )

2. _____ all the magazines on the shelf, there was one that was very interesting.
   - (A) Among
   - (B) By
   - (C) Between
   - (D) From   ( )

3. He said that his uncle _____ to see him the night before.
   - (A) had come
   - (B) came
   - (C) has come
   - (D) will come   ( )

4. I'm sure I _____ her two years ago.
   - (A) have seen
   - (B) saw
   - (C) will have seen
   - (D) had seen   ( )

5. _____ that our father were here to help us!
   - (A) Would
   - (B) May
   - (C) Could
   - (D) Should   ( )

6. You _____ such a large house. Your wife would have
been quite happy in a smaller house.
   - (A) need not buy
   - (B) needn't have bought
   - (C) will need to buy
   - (D) needed to buy   (   )

7. If you go near a camel, you risk _____.
   - (A) bitten
   - (B) is bitten
   - (C) being bitten
   - (D) having bitten   (   )

8. What sort of curtains do you think should _____ with
the carpet?
   - (A) go
   - (B) fit
   - (C) suit
   - (D) match   (   )

9. It's a long time since I saw him _____.
   - (A) later
   - (B) latter
   - (C) last
   - (D) latest   (   )

10. Lost things have a way of appearing when _____
expected.
   - (A) best
   - (B) least
   - (C) worst
   - (D) most   (   )

TEST 37 詳解

1. (**D**) She was able to go to college ***thanks to*** *the scholarship.*
幸虧有獎學金，她才能夠上大學。

> ***thanks to*** 幸虧；由於
> = ***owing to*** （這些片語為介系詞的片語，又稱「片語介系詞」，
> = ***because of*** 相當於介系詞。）

2. (**A**) ***Among*** *all the magazines on the shelf,* there was one
that was very interesting.
在架子上所有的雜誌中，有一本相當有趣。

> among 表「在～之中」，用於三者或三者以上；between 則指「二者之間」。
> shelf〔ʃɛlf〕*n.* 架子

3. (**A**) He ***said*** *that his uncle* ***had come*** *to see him the night before.*
他說他的叔叔前一晚來看過他。

> 比過去式更早發生的動作，須用「過去完成式」。

4. (**B**) I'm sure I ***saw*** *her* ***two years ago.***
我確定我二年前見過她。

> two years ago 和「過去簡單式」連用；凡表示過去某個時刻或某段時間，要用過去簡單式。

5. (**A**) ***Would*** *that our father were here to help us!*
要是父親在這裏幫我們就好了！

> ***Would that*** 接子句，表「不可能實現的願望」，子句中動詞用過去式 were，表與現在事實相反。***Would that = I wish***。（詳見文法寶典 p.370）

6. (**B**) You ***needn't have bought*** such a large house. Your wife would have been *quite* happy *in a smaller house.*

你不必買這麼大一間房子。你太太住小一點的房子就很高興了。

「***needn't have*** +過去分詞」，表「過去不必做但已做的事」。

$$\left.\begin{array}{l} \textit{\textbf{didn't need to}} \\ = \textit{\textbf{didn't have to}} \\ = \textit{\textbf{hadn't (got) to}} \end{array}\right\} + 原形動詞，「表過去不必做而未做的事」。$$

7. (**C**) *If you go near a camel,* you ***risk being bitten***.

如果你靠近一隻駱駝，會冒著被咬的危險。

risk「冒著～的危險」要接名詞或動名詞做受詞，由於句意為被動，所以要用「being + p.p.」。

8. (**A**) What sort of curtains *do you think* should ***go with*** the carpet? 你認為哪一種窗簾才搭配這塊地毯呢？

go with「搭配；適合」為片語用法，其他三個動詞 fit、suit、match 均為及物動詞，不必接介系詞。

sort (sort) *n.* 種類   curtain ('kɜtn̩) *n.* 窗簾
carpet ('kɑrpɪt) *n.* 地毯

9. (**C**) It's a long time *since I saw him* ***last***.

從我上次見到他，已是很久一段時間了。

later (後來) 和 latest (最新的) 指「時間」的先後；
latter (後者) 和 last (最後的) 指「順序」的先後。
It's a long time 是標準用法，It's been a long time 是通俗用法。

10. (**B**) Lost things have a way of appearing *when* ***least expected***.

遺失的東西常常在最意料不到時出現。

least 為負面意義的最高級，表「最少；最小；最不」；
worst 則表「最糟；最壞」。

TEST 38

Directions: *Of the four choices given after each sentence, choose the one most suitable for filling in the blank.*

1. As a statesman, Churchill was more successful than _____ I ever knew.

   (A) everyone
   (B) each one
   (C) anyone
   (D) no one   (   )

2. She is a lady, and will be treated _____.

   (A) as that
   (B) as such
   (C) like such
   (D) to such   (   )

3. The doctor decided to operate at once. The patient's condition _____ no delay.

   (A) allowed of
   (B) allowed for
   (C) thought of
   (D) thought about   (   )

4. _____ writer has dealt with the topic of "life and death."

   (A) Many
   (B) A lot of
   (C) Many a
   (D) A number of   (   )

5. I am wondering _____.

   (A) which house this belongs to
   (B) which house belongs to this
   (C) whose house this is
   (D) whose house is this   (   )

6. Pollution has reached _____ great an extent that we are barely able to cope with it.

   (A) much
   (B) many
   (C) so
   (D) such   (   )

7. When she saw all her children safe at home, her delight was _____ that she could not speak a word.

   (A) so
   (B) such
   (C) very much
   (D) great   (   )

8. He gave me clear directions and so I had no trouble _____ his office.

   (A) find
   (B) found
   (C) finding
   (D) to find   (   )

9. I _____ you last night, but I was too busy.

   (A) had to telephone
   (B) must have telephoned
   (C) should have telephoned
   (D) should telephone   (   )

10. Some day or _____ you will regret it.

    (A) another
    (B) ones
    (C) other
    (D) second   (   )

TEST 38 詳解

1. (**C**) *As a statesman,* Churchill was ***more*** successful ***than anyone***
I ever knew. 身爲政治家，邱吉爾比我所知道的任何人都成功。

　　「比較級＋***than anyone***」，表最高級。

　　statesman〔ˈstetsmən〕*n.* 政治家

2. (**B**) She is a lady, and will be treated ***as such.***
她是一位淑女，也會被像淑女般對待。

　　　such 可做代名詞，指「如此的人或事物」，在本句中，***as such*** 即指
as a lady。(詳見文法寶典 p.124)

3. (**A**) The doctor decided to operate *at once.* The patient's
condition ***allowed of*** no delay.
醫生決定要立刻動手術。病人的狀況不容延遲。

　　　allow of「容許」，allow for「考慮」，介系詞不同，意思不同，
(C) , (D) 必須以人做主詞。

　　　operate〔ˈɑpəˌret〕*v.* 動手術　　delay〔dɪˈle〕*n.* 延遲

4. (**C**) ***Many a*** writer has dealt with the topic *of "life and death."*
許多作家都已討論過「生與死」這個主題。

　　　　「***many a***＋單 N.＋單 V.」；「many＋複 N.＋複 V.」；
　　　　「a lot of＋複 N.＋複 V.」；「a number of＋複 N.＋複 V.」，
　　　　均表「許多」。(「many a＋單 N.＋單 V.」，卻表複數意義，詳見文法寶典 p.395)

5. (**C**) I am wondering ***whose house this is.***
我很想知道這棟房子是誰的。

　　　疑問形容詞 whose，加上所修飾的字，和疑問代名詞用法一樣，可引導名詞
子句，做 wondering 的受詞，在名詞子句中，whose house 又做 is 的補
語。名詞子句做受詞時，該用敘述型式，即「S.＋V.」，不可用疑問句型。
本題若用 belong to (屬於)，應改爲 whom this house belongs to。

6. (**C**) Pollution has reached *so great an extent that we are*

barely able to cope with it.

污染已達到如此大的程度，以致於我們幾乎無法應付。

> *so* 為副詞，*so* great an extent *that* 相當於 *such* a great
> extent *that*，表「如此～以致於」。
>
> extent〔 ɪk'stɛnt 〕*n.* 程度　　barely〔'bɛrlɪ 〕*adv.* 幾乎不 (= *hardly*)
> *cope with* 應付；處理 (= *deal with* = *handle*)

7. (**B**) *When she saw all her children safe at home,* her delight

was *such that she could not speak a word.*

當她看到她所有的孩子都平安無事待在家裡時，高興得說不出話來。

> *such～that*「如此～以致於」，such 為形容詞，後接名詞，也可
> 放在 be 動詞後，做主詞補語。
>
> delight〔 dɪ'laɪt 〕*n.* 高興；愉快

8. (**C**) He gave me clear directions and *so* I *had* no *trouble*

finding his office.

他給我的指示很清楚，所以我毫不費力就找到他的辦公室。

> *have* $\left\{ \begin{array}{l} \textit{trouble} \\ \textit{difficulty} \\ \textit{fun} \\ \textit{a good time} \end{array} \right.$ + (*in*) + *V-ing*
> （詳見文法寶典 p.444 ）
>
> direction〔 də'rɛkʃən 〕*n.* 方向；指示

9. (**C**) I *should have telephoned* you *last night,* but I was *too* busy.

我昨晚應該打電話你的，但是我太忙了。

> 「*should have* + *p.p.*」表「過去該做而未做」。

10. (**C**) *Some day or other* you will regret it. 你總有一天會後悔的。

> *some day or other* 總有一天；遲早 (= *sooner or later*)

TEST 39

Directions: *Of the four choices given after each sentence, choose the one most suitable for filling in the blank.*

1. I'm _____ excited to eat anything.
   - (A) enough
   - (B) hardly
   - (C) much
   - (D) too   ( )

2. Did the newspaper _____ it was going to rain?
   - (A) say
   - (B) talk
   - (C) tell
   - (D) write   ( )

3. After his explanation, she did not understand but became more _____.
   - (A) confused
   - (B) confusing
   - (C) understanding
   - (D) considerable   ( )

4. His theory is very difficult; _____ people understand it.
   - (A) little
   - (B) a little
   - (C) few
   - (D) a few   ( )

5. _____ at home, so their mother is left all alone.
   - (A) Either Tom or Mary lives
   - (B) Neither Tom nor Mary lives
   - (C) Both Tom and Mary live
   - (D) Both Tom and Mary don't live   ( )

6. Everyone liked her, and was glad _____ her company.
   - (A) having
   - (B) have
   - (C) to have
   - (D) had   (   )

7. The only method I know which will help you remember what you have heard at the lecture is _____ of keeping notes.
   - (A) some sort
   - (B) that
   - (C) the manner
   - (D) which   (   )

8. Were I wealthy, _____ I'm not, I would still go to work every day.
   - (A) so
   - (B) what
   - (C) which
   - (D) while   (   )

9. Reluctant as he was, he had no choice _____ to the other party's proposal.
   - (A) but agreeing
   - (B) to agree
   - (C) but agree
   - (D) but to agree   (   )

10. The thief ran away at the _____ of a policeman.
   - (A) screen
   - (B) scenery
   - (C) sight
   - (D) seeing   (   )

TEST 39 詳解

1.(**D**) I'm ***too*** excited *to eat anything.* 我太興奮了，吃不下任何東西。

　　too~to V.「太~以致於不」，本句也可說成：I'm ***so*** excited ***that I can't eat anything.***

2.(**A**) Did the newspaper ***say*** *it was going to rain*?
　　報上有說會下雨嗎？

　　　表「(報上)說；寫著」，動詞要用 ***say***，不可用 *write*。

3.(**A**) *After his explanation,* she did not understand but became

　　more confused. 在他解釋之後，她不但不懂，反而更困惑。

　　　confuse 是情感動詞，形容人「感到困惑的」要用 confused；形容事物「令人困惑的」，則用 confusing。
　　　understanding〔͵ʌndɚ'stændɪŋ〕*adj.* 體諒的
　　　considerable〔kən'sɪdərəbḷ〕*adj.* 相當多的

4.(**C**) His theory is *very* difficult; ***few*** people understand it.
　　他的理論非常難；很少人了解。

　　　　few 和 little 均表「很少」，有少到幾乎沒有的意味，相當於否定字；a few 和 a little 則為「一些」之意，沒有否定意味。few 和 a few 用於修飾可數名詞；little 和 a little 用於修飾不可數名詞。

5.(**B**) ***Neither*** Tom ***nor*** Mary lives at home, so their mother is

　　left *all alone.*
　　湯姆和瑪麗都不住在家裏，所以他們的母親獨自一人生活。

　　　　「***neither*** A ***nor*** B」表「二者皆非」；「either A or B」表「不是 A，就是 B」；「both A and B」表「二者皆是」。而若用「both A and B don't~」，表「部分否定」，指「一者是，一者不是」。

6. (**C**) Everyone liked her, and was glad *to have* her company.

人人都喜歡她，而且很高興有她作伴。

不定詞片語 to have her company 做副詞用，修飾 glad。
company〔'kʌmpənɪ〕*n.* 陪伴

7. (**B**) The only *method I know which will help you remember what you have heard at the lecture* is *that* of keeping notes.

我所知道，唯一能幫助你記住上課內容的方法，就是做筆記。

that 代替前面已經提過的單數名詞 the method，以避免重覆。
lecture〔'lɛktʃɚ〕*n.* 演講；講課　　*keep notes* 做筆記

8. (**C**) Were I wealthy, *which I'm not,* I would *still* go to work every day. 如果我很富有，不過我不是，我還是會每天去上班。

先行詞為 wealthy，關代要用 which；Were I wealthy 原為 *If I were wealthy*，為與現在事實相反的假設語氣。

9. (**D**) *Reluctant as he was,* he *had no choice but to* agree to the other party's proposal.

雖然他不願意，但他除了同意對方的提議外，別無選擇。

have no choice but + *to V.* 除了～之外別無選擇
cannot choose but + *V.* 不得不
reluctant〔rɪ'lʌktənt〕*adj.* 不願意的
party〔'partɪ〕*n.* 一方　　proposal〔prə'pozḷ〕*n.* 提議

10. (**C**) The thief ran away *at the sight of* a policeman.

小偷一看到警察就逃走了。

at the sight of 一看到（*at the sound of* 一聽見）
screen〔skrin〕*n.* 螢幕　　scenery〔'sinərɪ〕*n.* 風景

TEST 40

Directions: *Of the four choices given after each sentence, choose the one most suitable for filling in the blank.*

1. Among the guests _____ to the party were two foreign ladies.
   - (A) invite
   - (B) invited
   - (C) inviting
   - (D) who invited   (   )

2. How long _____ here by the end of next year?
   - (A) will you work
   - (B) are you working
   - (C) you will have worked
   - (D) will you have been working   (   )

3. The picture was wonderful. You _____ to have seen it.
   - (A) ought
   - (B) should
   - (C) have
   - (D) had   (   )

4. I am very regretful for _____ I said to her yesterday.
   - (A) that
   - (B) whether
   - (C) what
   - (D) which   (   )

5. The window was _____ see through.
   - (A) enough dirty to
   - (B) so dirty that you can
   - (C) so dirty to
   - (D) too dirty to   (   )

6. Most of the job is complete, but a few things _____ done.

    (A) have remain to be

    (B) remain to be

    (C) are remained to be

    (D) are remaining to be   ( )

7. No doubt Mary is wrong, but I would rather _____ too much, since nobody is perfect.

    (A) you not to pick on her

    (B) you didn't pick on her

    (C) you not picking on her

    (D) you don't pick on her   ( )

8. My students were few in number, _____ four or five altogether.

    (A) as many as

    (B) as little as

    (C) no less than

    (D) no more than   ( )

9. The next train will be _____ crowded than this one.

    (A) much

    (B) a little

    (C) as

    (D) less   ( )

10. I saw two tall figures _____ slowly in the dusk.

    (A) walked

    (B) to walk

    (C) walking

    (D) be walking   ( )

TEST 40 詳解

1. (**B**) Among the guests *invited to the party* were two foreign ladies.

   在受邀參加舞會的客人中，有二位來自外國的女士。

   本句原為形容詞子句 *who were invited to*…，修飾先行詞 guests，省略 who were 而形成分詞片語。

2. (**D**) How long <u>will you have been working</u> here *by the end of next year*?

   到了明年年底，你將在此工作多久了呢？

   「未來完成進行式」可表「到未來某時，已經完成並且動作可能繼續」。

3. (**A**) The picture was wonderful. You ***ought to*** have seen it.

   那幅畫很棒，你應該看看。

   ought to = ***should***，後接「have + p.p.」，表「過去該做而未做」。

4. (**C**) I am *very* regretful for ***what*** *I said to her yesterday.*

   我對我昨天向她說的話後悔不已。

   複合關代 what，引導名詞子句，做介系詞 for 的受詞，在名詞子句中，what 又做 said 的受詞，what = the thing that。

5. (**D**) The window was ***too*** dirty ***to*** *see through.*

   這窗戶太髒了，無法看透。

   too ~ ***to*** V. 表「太~以致於不」；so ~ that 表「如此~以致於」，但 that 子句應改為 that you can't see it through。

6. (**B**) Most of the job is complete, but a few things *__remain to__*
__be done__. 這個工作大部份已完成，但還有一些事要做。

> *__remain to be done__* 有待被做
> *__remain to be seen__* 有待觀察
> remain 和 seem 一樣，無進行式。(詳見文法寶典 p.343)

7. (**B**) *No doubt* Mary is wrong, but *I would rather you didn't*
pick on her *too much*, *since nobody is perfect.*
無疑地瑪麗是錯的，但我希望你不要過於批評她，因為沒有人是完美的。

> *I would rather* = *I wish*，子句中用過去式，表示與現在事實相
> 反的願望。
> *pick on* 批評　　perfect〔'pɝfɪkt〕*adj.* 完美的

8. (**D**) My students were few *in number,* *__no more than__* *four or*
five altogether. 我的學生人數很少，總共只有四、五個。

> *__no more than__* 僅僅 (= *only*)
> *__no less than__* 多達 (= *as many as*)
> no 在比較級形容詞前，等於 not at all。如 *no more than*「一點
> 也不超過」，即「僅僅」。(詳見文法寶典 p.202)
> altogether〔͵ɔltə'gɛðɚ〕*adv.* 總計

9. (**D**) The next train will be *__less__* crowded *than this one.*
下一班火車會比這一班不擠。

> 「less + 原級」為「負面比較」，表「比較不」；
> 「正面比較」則用「more + 原級或～er」。

10. (**C**) I *saw* two tall figures *__walking__* *slowly in the dusk.*
我看見二個高高的身影緩緩走在薄暮中。

> see 為感官動詞，可接原形動詞或現在分詞，做受詞補語，接現在
> 分詞則強調動作的進行。
> figure〔'fɪgɚ〕*n.* 人影　　dusk〔dʌsk〕*n.* 薄暮；黃昏

TEST 41

Directions: *Of the four choices given after each sentence, choose the one most suitable for filling in the blank.*

1. Changes have taken place in many areas of our life, especially in _____ related to housing and employment.
   - (A) it
   - (B) that
   - (C) these
   - (D) those   (   )

2. _____ of a novelist, he has the ability to make acute observations of people.
   - (A) As may be expected
   - (B) Judging
   - (C) As a viewpoint
   - (D) Viewing   (   )

3. My sister _____ here by now, for she took the early train.
   - (A) must arrive
   - (B) can arrive
   - (C) may arrive
   - (D) ought to have arrived   (   )

4. He wanted to succeed even at the _____ of his health.
   - (A) danger
   - (B) service
   - (C) expense
   - (D) mercy   (   )

5. It is yet _____ whether this plan will succeed or not.
   - (A) impossible
   - (B) unfinished
   - (C) much to do
   - (D) to be seen   (   )

6. Please return the book when you _____ reading it.

   (A) finished
   (B) had finished
   (C) will finish
   (D) have finished   (   )

7. I don't mind lending you the money _____ you pay it back
   within a year.

   (A) which
   (B) supposed
   (C) whether
   (D) provided   (   )

8. _____ for the support of the public, the President could
   not have survived the revolt.

   (A) But
   (B) If it were
   (C) Unless
   (D) Without   (   )

9. He is so wise that he knows better.
   = He is _____ wise not to know better.

   (A) enough
   (B) so
   (C) too
   (D) very   (   )

10. He kissed the lady _____ the hand to show his respect.

    (A) on
    (B) by
    (C) at
    (D) with   (   )

TEST 41 詳解

1. (**D**) Changes have taken place *in many areas of our life,*

   *especially in **those** related to housing and employment.*
   我們的生活中有許多方面都改變了，特別是關於居住和就業方面。

   > those 在此代替前面已出現過的 the areas，其後省略了 which are。
   > ***be related to*** 與～有關　　employment〔ɪmˈplɔɪmənt〕*n.* 就業

2. (**A**) ***As may be expected*** *of a novelist,* he has the ability to

   make acute observations of people.
   他對人們具有敏銳的觀察能力，這正是一位小說家會被期待應具備的。

   > as 為準關代，引導形容詞子句，修飾後面整句話，as 代替後面 he
   > has…people 整句話，在形容詞子句中做主詞。(詳見文法寶典 p.160)
   > acute〔əˈkjut〕*adj.* 敏銳的　　observation〔͵ɑbzəˈveʃən〕*n.* 觀察

3. (**D**) My sister ***ought to have*** arrived here *by now*, for she
   took the early train.
   我姐姐現在應該已經要到達此地了，因為她搭早班火車。

   > 「***ought to have + p.p***」，表「過去應做而未做」，ought to = should。
   > ***by now*** 此時 (= *by this time*)

4. (**C**) He wanted to succeed *even at the **expense** of his health.*
   即使犧牲了健康，他也要成功。

   > ***at the expense of*** 犧牲；付出～代價
   > (A) 應用 run the danger of「冒～危險」；(B) at a person's service
   > 「隨時為某人服務」；(D) at the mercy of「任由～擺佈」，均不合句意。

5 (**D**) It ***is yet to be seen*** *whether this plan will succeed or not.*
   這個計畫是否會成功還有待觀察。

   > 「***be yet to be + p.p.***」 = 「***remain to be + p.p.***」，表「有待被」。

6. (**D**) Please return the book *when you **have finished** reading it.*
當你讀完這本書，請歸還。

> 表示到未來某時即將完成的動作，本應用未來完成式，但本句爲表時間的副詞子句，不能用 will，要用現在完成式代替未來完成式。

7. (**D**) I don't mind lending you the money ***provided** you pay it back within a year.* 如果你在一年內歸還，我不介意借你這筆錢。

> ***provided*** 表「如果」（ = *if*)，也可用 providing、suppose、supposing，爲表條件的副詞子句連接詞。不可用 *supposed*。
> （詳見文法寶典 p.365）

8. (**A**) ***But for** the support of the public,* the President could not have survived the revolt.
如果沒有群眾的支持，總統就無法逃過這場叛亂。

> ***but for** = **without***，表「如果沒有」，沒有時態之分；若用子句，「***If it were not for*~** 」爲「與現在事實相反」的用法；「If it had not been for~」則爲「與過去事實相反」的用法。
> survive〔sə'vaɪv〕*v.* 存活；生還　　revolt〔rɪ'volt〕*n.* 叛亂

9. (**C**) He is *so* wise *that he knows better.*

= He is *too* wise *not to know better.*
他非常聰明，不會上當。

> ***know better*** 懂得很清楚；不致於笨到如此程度；不會上當
> 「***too*~*not to*+*V.*」是雙重否定，表「非常~，不會不…」。

10. (**A**) He *kissed* the lady ***on the hand*** *to show his respect.*
他吻了那位小姐的手，以示尊敬。

> 及物動詞的受詞若爲人身體的某一部位，要用「動詞＋人＋介系詞＋the＋部位」，如本題 *kiss* the lady *on the* hand，*grab* the thief *by the* arm 等。（詳見文法寶典 p.277）

TEST 42

Directions: *Of the four choices given after each sentence, choose the one most suitable for filling in the blank.*

1. These part-timers are paid _____ hour.
   (A) in the
   (B) in an
   (C) by the
   (D) by an   (   )

2. Philosophy is not _____ as you imagine it is.
   (A) so difficult subject
   (B) so a difficult subject
   (C) a so difficult subject
   (D) so difficult a subject   (   )

3. John is _____ of the two boys.
   (A) taller
   (B) the taller
   (C) tallest
   (D) the tallest   (   )

4. He is a great inventor and is called _____ of the age.
   (A) Edisons
   (B) an Edison
   (C) the Edison
   (D) Edison   (   )

5. _____ who insults himself will be insulted by others.
   (A) That
   (B) He
   (C) Those
   (D) Which   (   )

6. You can borrow two books _____ condition that you bring them back within a week.

   (A) at
   (B) with
   (C) by
   (D) on   (   )

7. In the park, _____ sat on benches and others strolled about.

   (A) boys
   (B) many
   (C) people
   (D) some   (   )

8. Farmers are always _____ the weather.

   (A) at the mercy of
   (B) depended on
   (C) dependent in
   (D) merciful of   (   )

9. After a long walk in the sun, I was overcome _____.

   (A) with the thirst
   (B) with thirsty
   (C) by the thirst
   (D) by thirsty   (   )

10. I _____ reading for an hour when he came in.

   (A) was
   (B) have been
   (C) had been
   (D) will be   (   )

TEST 42 詳解

1. (**C**) These part-timers are paid *by the hour*.
這些兼差者按時計薪。

> *by the hour* 以鐘點計（詳見文法寶典 p.566）
> part-timer (ˈpɑrtˈtaɪmɚ) *n.* 兼差者

2. (**D**) Philosophy is *not* so difficult a subject *as you imagine it is*.
哲學並不像你所想像是那麼難的一個科目。

> *not as…as*「不像～那樣」，表不同等的比較，you imagine 為插入語。
> 本題考不定冠詞 a 的位置，so, as, too, how + 形容詞 + a + 名詞。（詳見文法寶典 p.216）
> philosophy (fəˈlɑsəfɪ) *n.* 哲學

3. (**B**) John is *the taller of the two boys*.
約翰是二個男孩中比較高的。

> 表示「二者中比較～的」，比較級前要加 the。

4. (**C**) He is a great inventor *and* is called *the Edison of the age*.
他是一位偉大的發明家，被稱為當代的愛迪生。

> 專有名詞原則上不加冠詞，但有修飾語限制時，須加冠詞。
> *of the age* 當代的

5. (**B**) *He who insults himself* will be insulted *by others*.
人必自侮而後人侮之。

> 「*He who* + 單 *V.*」相當於「*Those who* + 複 *V.*」，表「凡是～的人」。
> insult (ɪnˈsʌlt) *v.* 侮辱

6. (**D**) You can borrow two books **_on condition that_** *you bring*

them back within a week.

只要你能在一週內歸還，你就可以借二本書。

> **_on condition that_** = *if*
> condition (kən'dɪʃən) *n.* 條件

7. (**D**) *In the park,* **_some_** *sat on benches* and **_others_** *strolled about.*

在公園裏，有些人坐在長椅上，有些人到處閒逛。

> 表「有些～，有些…」，代名詞用「some～others…」，或「some～
> some…」。
> bench (bɛntʃ) *n.* 長椅   stroll (strol) *v.* 閒逛

8. (**A**) Farmers are *always* **_at the mercy of_** the weather.

農夫總是受天氣的擺佈。

> **_be at the mercy of_** 受～的擺佈
> **_depend on_** 依賴 (要用主動) (= *be dependent on*)
> merciful ('mɜsɪfəl) *adj.* 慈悲的；寬大的

9. (**C**) *After a long walk in the sun,* I *was overcome* **_by the thirst._**

在太陽下走了很久之後，我快渴死了。

> 「**_be overcome by_**」表「被～克服、擊敗」，其後應接名詞。
> thirst (θɜst) *n.* 口渴   thirsty ('θɜstɪ) *adj.* 口渴的
> **_thirsty_**，**_guilty_** 看起來是名詞，其實是形容詞，所以常考。

10. (**C**) I **_had been_** reading *for an hour when he came in.*

當他進來時，我已經看了一小時的書了。

> 表「從過去稍早進行至過去某時，且強調該動作仍繼續進行」，用
> 「過去完成進行式」。

TEST 43

Directions: *Of the four choices given after each sentence, choose the one most suitable for filling in the blank.*

1. We have plenty of bread, so I _____ buy a loaf.
   (A) needn't to
   (B) must not
   (C) haven't to
   (D) don't need to ( )

2. As the summer vacation nears, I'm looking forward _____ my friends.
   (A) to meet
   (B) to meeting
   (C) for meeting
   (D) to be meeting ( )

3. The wall wasn't _____ dogs out.
   (A) high enough to keep
   (B) so high as keep
   (C) higher than to keep
   (D) so high that can keep ( )

4. You are _____ to gain weight in summer than in winter because you tend to lose your appetite when it is hot.
   (A) less likely
   (B) less unlikely
   (C) very likely
   (D) very unlikely ( )

5. _____ are very sociable people. They love to give parties very often.
   (A) The Johnson
   (B) Johnson
   (C) The Johnsons
   (D) Johnsons ( )

6. Come over and see me _____ tomorrow.
   - (A) sometime
   - (B) some time
   - (C) sometimes
   - (D) some times   (   )

7. My father _____ that we should go camping.
   - (A) invited
   - (B) talked
   - (C) told
   - (D) suggested   (   )

8. Judy _____ me that she would come to our party tonight.
   - (A) said
   - (B) spoke
   - (C) talked
   - (D) told   (   )

9. Study is necessary, and so is practice. The combination will give one the ability to communicate in a foreign language, but _____ will result in slow, incorrect speech.
   - (A) all of them
   - (B) both of them
   - (C) none of them
   - (D) either one of them alone   (   )

10. We honor him for _____ he is, not for _____ he has.
   - (A) that
   - (B) what
   - (C) which
   - (D) how   (   )

TEST 43 詳解

1. (**D**) We have plenty of bread, *so* I <u>don't need to</u> buy a loaf.
我們有很多麵包，所以我不必再買了。

$$\begin{cases} \textbf{\textit{needn't}} + V. & 不必；不需要 \\ = \textbf{\textit{don't need to}} + V. \\ = \textbf{\textit{don't have to}} + V. \end{cases}$$

「must not」作「不可以」解，表禁止。
loaf〔lof〕*n.* 一條（麵包）

2. (**B**) *As the summer vacation nears*, I'm **looking forward to meeting** my friends. 隨著暑假的接近，我期待見到我的朋友。

look forward to「期待」，to 為介系詞，要接名詞或動名詞做受詞。

3. (**A**) The wall wasn't <u>high **enough to keep** dogs out</u>.
這面牆不夠高，無法阻止狗跳進來。

「**enough to** + V.」（足以）表肯定的結果；「**too~to** + V.」（太~而不能）
則表否定的結果，二者皆是相關修飾詞，會成對出現。(詳見文法寶典 p.417)

4. (**A**) You **are** **less** **likely** **to** gain weight *in summer than in winter because you tend to lose your appetite when it is hot.*
在夏天比在冬天不可能變胖，因為天氣熱容易失去食慾。

依句意為負面比較，要用「**less** + 原級」。
「**be likely to** + V.」表「可能」。
tend to + V. 傾向於；容易　　appetite〔'æpə,taɪt〕*n.* 食慾

5. (**C**) **The Johnsons** are *very* sociable people. They love to give parties *very often*.
強森一家人都非常善於交際。他們常喜歡舉辦宴會。

表「姓~的一家人」，姓氏要加 S 且要加 the。*the Johnsons* 指「強森一家人」。　　sociable〔'soʃəbḷ〕*adj.* 善交際的

6. (**A**) Come over and see me *sometime* tomorrow.
   明天找個時間來看我。

   > *sometime* 某個時間　　*some time* 一段時間
   > *sometimes* 偶爾；有時　　*some times* 幾次 (= *several times*)
   > 這條題目常考，很重要。(詳見文法寶典 p.259)

7. (**D**) My father *suggested that* we *should* go camping.
   父親建議我們去露營。

   > order
   > suggest
   > insist　　} that + S. + (should) + 原 V.
   > demand　　(詳見文法寶典 p.372)

8. (**D**) Judy *told* me *that she would come to our party tonight.*
   茱蒂告訴我,她今晚會來參加我們的舞會。

   > 此四個動詞只有 tell 可直接接人做受詞,say,speak,和 talk 都
   > 要用 to *sb.*。

9. (**D**) Study is necessary, and *so* is practice. The combination will
   give one the ability *to communicate in a foreign language*,
   but either one of them *alone* will result in slow, incorrect
   speech.
   讀書是必要的,而練習也是。二者結合,可給予一個人用外語溝通的
   能力,但只有其一,會導致說話慢且不正確。

   > all 或 none 用於三者或三者以上皆是或皆不是;both 用於二者皆
   > 是,either 則用於二者之一。

10. (**B**) We honor him *for what he is, not for what he has.*
    我們尊敬他是因為他的人品,而不是因為他的財富。

    > 「*what one is*」指「某人現在的樣子;某人今日的成就」;
    > 「*what one has*」指「某人的財產」。

TEST 44

Directions: *Of the four choices given after each sentence, choose the one most suitable for filling in the blank.*

1. _____ he is wealthy, he is not content.
   (A) With all
   (B) For all
   (C) In spite of
   (D) Despite   (   )

2. The teacher as well as the students _____ to study hard.
   (A) are expected
   (B) expected
   (C) expect
   (D) is expected   (   )

3. Billiards _____ a good and interesting indoor game.
   (A) is
   (B) are
   (C) has
   (D) have   (   )

4. When I get home, my wife will probably _____ television.
   (A) have been watched
   (B) watched
   (C) watch
   (D) be watching   (   )

5. It is a pity that he _____ miss such a good opportunity.
   (A) could
   (B) should
   (C) would
   (D) must   (   )

6. We _____ Tom honest.
   (A) see
   (B) expect
   (C) regard
   (D) consider   (   )

7. The wind was not _____ to prevent us from sky-diving.
   (A) as strong
   (B) as strong as
   (C) so strong
   (D) so strong as   (   )

8. The guests _____ the happy couple a long and prosperous life.
   (A) hoped
   (B) wanted
   (C) supposed
   (D) wished   (   )

9. It was at this bookstore _____ I met my future wife.
   (A) which
   (B) that
   (C) this
   (D) here   (   )

10. The train makes several stops _____ Taipei and Taichung.
    (A) between
    (B) from
    (C) among
    (D) beside   (   )

TEST 44 詳解

1.(**B**) ***For all*** *he is wealthy,* he is not content.
　　儘管他很富有，他並不滿足。

　　　四個選項均表「儘管」，但 (A)、(C)、(D) 為介系詞用法，只能接名詞
　　　做受詞，而 for all 可接名詞，for all (that) 也可視為連接詞，接子句。
　　　（一定要看文法寶典 p.530 ）
　　　content〔kən'tɛnt〕*adj.* 滿足的

2.(**D**) ***The teacher*** *as well as the students* ***is*** <u>expected</u> to study hard.
　　老師和學生一樣要努力用功。

　　　「as well as」是對等連接詞，在此連接二個主詞，因為強調前者，
　　　故動詞應與前者一致。在本題中，「老師和學生一樣」，重點強調「老師」。

3.(**A**) Billiards ***is*** a good and interesting indoor game.
　　撞球是一種很好、很有趣的室內遊戲。

　　　billiards〔'bɪljədz〕*n.* 撞球，看起來是複數，但意義上為單數，許多
　　　學科名稱也是如此，如 mathematics（數學），politics（政治學），
　　　physics（物理學）等。要特別注意字尾有 s 的單數名詞。

4.(**D**) ***When I get home****,* my wife ***will*** *probably* ***be watching***
　　television.
　　當我到家時，我太太可能正在看電視。

　　　表「未來某時正在進行的動作」，用「未來進行式」。

5.(**B**) ***It is a pity that*** *he* ***should*** *miss such a good opportunity.*
　　他竟然錯過這麼好的機會，真可惜。

$$
It\ is\ \begin{cases} \textit{a pity} \\ \textit{strange} \\ \textit{surprising} \end{cases} that + S. + \textit{should} + 原 V.\quad （should 表「竟然」）
$$
　　　　　　　　　　　　　　　　　　　　　　　　　（詳見文法寶典 p.375）

6. (**D**) We ***consider*** Tom honest.

我們認為湯姆很誠實。

> consider（認為）接受詞後，句意仍不完整，要加受詞補語，補語原為 to be honest，to be 可省略，亦可保留；see 和 regard 亦表「認為」，但補語要用 as honest。(B) 應用 We expect Tom to be honest. (我們希望湯姆要誠實。)

7. (**D**) The wind was not *so* strong *as to prevent us from sky-diving.*

風勢並沒有強到足以阻止我們去跳傘。

> ***so ~ as to + V.*** 如此～以致於
> （本題不是表「比較」，是表「結果」，詳見文法寶典 p.416）
> sky-diving〔'skaɪˌdaɪvɪŋ〕 *n.* 高空跳傘特技運動

8. (**D**) The guests ***wished*** the happy couple a long and
　　　　　　　　　　　　　　　間　接　受　詞　　　　直　　接
prosperous life.
　　受　　詞

賓客們祝福這對快樂的夫妻長壽並且好運連連。

> ***wish*** 可作「祝福」解，為授與動詞，後接人和祝福內容二個受詞。
> couple〔'kʌpḷ〕 *n.* 一對（夫妻、男女朋友）
> prosperous〔'prɑspərəs〕 *adj.* 繁榮的；好運的

9. (**B**) ***It was*** at this bookstore ***that*** *I met my future wife.*

就是在這家書店，我遇見了我未來的太太。

> 本句話為強調句型，其結構為：
> 「***It is / was*** + 強調部分 + ***that*** + 其餘部分」，強調部分為地方時，也可用 where 代替 that。(一定要詳閱文法寶典 p.115)

10. (**A**) The train makes several stops ***between*** Taipei and Taichung.

火車在台北和台中之間停好幾次。

> ***between*** 表「二者之間」；among 則用於「三者或三者以上的受詞之間」。

TEST 45

Directions: *Of the four choices given after each sentence, choose the one most suitable for filling in the blank.*

1. Science is far _____ a collection of facts and methods.
   - (A) away from
   - (B) down from
   - (C) less as
   - (D) more than   (   )

2. He is _____ of a musician.
   - (A) anybody
   - (B) anything
   - (C) somebody
   - (D) something   (   )

3. The hairdresser now cuts _____ men's and women's hair.
   - (A) either
   - (B) both
   - (C) each
   - (D) any   (   )

4. He is _____ is called a self-made man.
   - (A) that
   - (B) which
   - (C) what
   - (D) who   (   )

5. Living _____ I do so remote from town, I rarely meet people.
   - (A) where
   - (B) as
   - (C) while
   - (D) if   (   )

6. The train was running _____ full speed.

    (A) at
    (B) with
    (C) by
    (D) in   (   )

7. _____ present at the meeting supported the bill.

    (A) These
    (B) That
    (C) Those
    (D) They   (   )

8. His warning _____ by the villagers.

    (A) was paid no attention
    (B) was paid no attention to
    (C) paid no attention
    (D) paid no attention to   (   )

9. It is necessary that every member _____ acquaint himself with the rules of the club as soon as possible.

    (A) would
    (B) might
    (C) should
    (D) could   (   )

10. He did his best; otherwise he _____ the first prize.

    (A) cannot win
    (B) would have won
    (C) will not have won
    (D) would not have won   (   )

TEST 45 詳解

1. (**D**) Science is *far **more than*** a collection *of facts and methods*.
科學絕不只是事實和方法的蒐集而已。

> 「***more than***」表「不只是」，far 可加強比較級和最高級的程度。
> 「far away from」表「離～很遠」，不合句意。

2. (**D**) He *is **something of a*** musician.
他有點音樂家的樣子。

> ***be something of a*** 有一點～的樣子；可以說是一個

3. (**B**) The hairdresser *now* cuts ***both*** men's *and* women's hair.
這位美髮師現在男士女士的頭髮都剪。

> ***both～and*** 是對等連接詞，men's 後省了 hair。
> hairdresser ('hɛr,drɛsɚ) *n.* 美髮師

4. (**C**) He is ***what is called*** a self-made man.
他就是所謂白手起家的人。

> ***what is called***「所謂的」，也可寫成 ***what we call*** 或 ***what you
> call***，是插入語，和句子其他部分無文法關連。
> self-made ('sɛlf'med) *adj.* 靠自己努力成功的

5. (**B**) *Living **as I do** so remote from town*, I *rarely* meet people.
我住得離城鎮如此的遙遠，所以很少遇到別人。

> 「現在 (過去) 分詞 + *as one* + *does* (*is*) + 主要子句」，為加強語氣的
> 副詞子句，在此表原因，do 在此即代替動詞 live。as I do 為插入語，
> 前後亦可加逗號。(詳見文法寶典 p.530)
> remote (rɪ'mot) *adj.* 遠離的；遙遠的

6. (**A**) The train was running ***at*** *full speed*. 火車全速前進。

> 表「以～速度」介系詞用 ***at***。例：The bus runs ***at*** the rate of 40 miles an hour. (詳見文法寶典 p.557)

7. (**C**) ***Those*** *present at the meeting* supported the bill.
   與會者都支持這項法案。

> those present 相當於 those *who were* present，指「出席的人；在場的人。」***those who = the people who***，是固定用法。
> present〔'prɛznt〕*adj.* 出席的；在場的　　bill〔bɪl〕*n.* 法案

8. (**B**) His warning ***was paid no attention to*** *by the villagers*.
   他的警告村民毫不注意。

> ***pay attention to*** 的被動是 ***be paid attention to***，to 不可省略。
> villager〔'vɪlɪdʒɚ〕*n.* 村民

9. (**C**) ***It is necessary that*** every member ***should*** acquaint himself with the rules of the club as soon as possible.
   每位會員必須要儘快熟悉俱樂部裏的規定。

> *It is* $\left\{ \begin{array}{l} \textbf{\textit{necessary}} \\ \textbf{\textit{important}} \\ \textbf{\textit{natural}} \end{array} \right\}$ *that* + *S.* + (*should*) + 原 *V.* (詳見文法寶典 p.374)
>
> ***acquaint oneself with*** 熟悉

10. (**D**) He did his best; *otherwise* he would not have won the first prize.
    他盡了全力；否則，他就不會得到第一名。

> 後半句為「與過去事實相反」的假設語氣，故用 would not have won，otherwise 代替一個 if 子句。(詳見文法寶典 p.367)
> prize〔praɪz〕*n.* 獎；獎品

TEST 46

Directions: *Of the four choices given after each sentence, choose the one most suitable for filling in the blank.*

1. His beard made him look older _____ ten years.
   - (A) by
   - (B) with
   - (C) to
   - (D) in   (   )

2. Spaghetti and meat sauce _____ one of my favorite dishes.
   - (A) are
   - (B) is
   - (C) were
   - (D) be   (   )

3. She was seen _____ the room.
   - (A) enter
   - (B) entered
   - (C) be entered
   - (D) to enter   (   )

4. His salary is _____ what it was seven years ago.
   - (A) double
   - (B) as double
   - (C) by double
   - (D) for double   (   )

5. You can't vote _____ you have satisfied all the formal conditions.
   - (A) until
   - (B) when
   - (C) whenever
   - (D) since   (   )

6. Only after the accident _____ have his car inspected.

   (A) had he
   (B) he had
   (C) did he
   (D) he did   (   )

7. Science as _____ is not primarily interested in the value or worth of things.

   (A) itself
   (B) known
   (C) seen
   (D) such   (   )

8. She studied hard with a _____ to becoming a teacher of Japanese.

   (A) means
   (B) purpose
   (C) hope
   (D) view   (   )

9. I was not in the _____ surprised at what he said.

   (A) last
   (B) all
   (C) least
   (D) latest   (   )

10. It has been _____ hot these days.

   (A) steam
   (B) steaming
   (C) steamed
   (D) steamy   (   )

TEST 46 詳解

1. (**A**) His beard made him look older *by ten years*.

他的鬍子使他看起來老了十歲。

表示「差距」，介系詞用 *by*。

例：He is taller than I *by* three inches. (詳見文法寶典 p.566)

beard〔bɪrd〕*n.* 鬍子

2. (**B**) Spaghetti and meat sauce *is* one of my favorite dishes.

義大利肉醬麵是我最喜歡的菜色之一。

spaghetti and meat sauce「義大利肉醬麵」為一種食物，故用單數動詞。

spaghetti〔spəˈgɛtɪ〕*n.* 義大利麵

3. (**D**) She *was seen to* enter the room.

她被看到進入該房間。

感官動詞的被動語態，要用帶 to 的不定詞來做主詞補語。(詳見文法寶典 p.381)

4. (**A**) His salary is *double* what it was *seven years ago*.

他的薪水是七年前的二倍。

倍數表達法：「倍數 + as ~ as…」或「倍數 + 名詞片語」。(詳見文法寶典 p.181)

5. (**A**) You ca*n't* vote *until* you have satisfied *all the formal conditions*.

直到你符合所有正式的條件後，你才能投票。

「*not ~ until*」表「直到…才」。選項 (B)、(C)、(D) 皆不合句意。

vote〔vot〕*v.* 投票   satisfy〔ˈsætɪsˌfaɪ〕*v.* 滿足；符合

formal〔ˈfɔrml̩〕*adj.* 正式的   condition〔kənˈdɪʃən〕*n.* 情況；條件

6. (**C**) *Only after the accident did he* have his car inspected.

　只有在那件意外發生後，他才叫人檢查他的車子。

$$Only + \begin{cases} 副詞子句 \\ 副詞片語 \end{cases} + 助動詞 + 主詞，為倒裝句型。$$

　　inspect〔ɪn'spɛkt〕*v.* 檢查

7. (**D**) Science *as such* is not *primarily* interested in the value or worth *of things*.

　科學本身的主要興趣不在於事物的價值。

　　such 在此做代名詞，指「如此的人或事物」。*as such* 在此相當於 *in itself*，作「本身」解。(詳見文法寶典 p.124)

　　primarily〔'praɪ,mɛrəlɪ〕*adv.* 主要地

8. (**D**) She studied hard *with a view to becoming a teacher of*

　Japanese. 她用功讀書，想成為一位日文老師。

　　with a view to = *with an eye to* = *with the purpose of* = *in the hope of*，後接動名詞，表目的。

9. (**C**) I was *not in the least* surprised *at what he said.*

　我對於他所說的一點也不感到驚訝。

　　not in the least 一點也不 (= *not at all*)

10. (**B**) It has been *steaming* hot *these days.*

　這幾天快熱死了。

　　少數分詞可當副詞，加強形容詞的程度。steaming 修飾 hot，表示「非常熱；酷熱」。(詳見文法寶典 p.455)

　　steam〔stim〕*n.* 蒸氣　*v.* 蒸

　　steamy〔'stimɪ〕*adj.* 蒸氣般的；霧濛濛的

TEST 47

Directions: *Of the four choices given after each sentence, choose the one most suitable for filling in the blank.*

1. _____ the recent political corruption, the minister had to resign.
   (A) As
   (B) As a result
   (C) Because
   (D) Because of   (   )

2. By the age of 25, she _____ in five different countries.
   (A) has lived
   (B) had lived
   (C) lives
   (D) lived   (   )

3. My father insisted that I _____ go to see the place.
   (A) might
   (B) ought
   (C) should
   (D) would   (   )

4. We make cotton _____ many useful things.
   (A) of
   (B) out of
   (C) into
   (D) from   (   )

5. It is no _____ arguing about it, because he will never change his mind.
   (A) use
   (B) help
   (C) time
   (D) while   (   )

6. There _____ no bus service, I had to take a taxi.
   (A) is
   (B) be
   (C) being
   (D) been   (   )

7. "Would you pass me the salt?" "_____."
   (A) Here are you
   (B) Here you are
   (C) Here is it
   (D) Here are they   (   )

8. Let's go to the movies together, _____?
   (A) shall we
   (B) will you
   (C) don't we
   (D) won't you   (   )

9. This vacuum cleaner is highly recommended for _____
   durability.
   (A) its
   (B) it's
   (C) it is
   (D) that   (   )

10. Tom and Joe look alike. I always mistake one _____
    the other.
    (A) from
    (B) with
    (C) of
    (D) for   (   )

TEST 47 詳解

1. (**D**) ***Because of*** *the recent political corruption,* the minister had to resign.
   由於最近的政治舞弊事件，部長只得辭職。

   > as 和 because 為連接詞，須接子句，***because of*** 和 ***as a result of*** 接名詞。
   > political〔pə'lıtık!〕*adj.* 政治的
   > corruption〔kə'rʌpʃən〕*n.* 貪污；舞弊
   > minister〔'mınıstə〕*n.* 部長

2. (**B**) *By the age of 25,* she <u>had lived</u> *in five different countries.*
   她到二十五歲時，已經住過五個不同的國家。

   > 表到過去某時已經完成的動作，用過去完成式。

3. (**C**) My father ***insisted*** that *I* ***should*** *go to see the place.*
   父親堅持我應該去看看那個地方。

   > insist〔ın'sıst〕*v.* 堅持，為慾望動詞，that 子句中助動詞要用 should。

4. (**C**) We ***make*** cotton ***into*** many useful things.
   我們把棉花做成許多有用的東西。

   > 「***make*** A ***into*** B」表「把 A 做成 B」，A 為材料，B 為成品。
   > 亦可用「B be made of A」、「B be made out of A」，或「B be made from A」，表「B 是由 A 製成」。

5. (**A**) ***It is no*** <u>***use***</u> arguing about it, *because he will never change his mind.*
   爭辯也沒有用，因為他絕不會改變心意。

   > ***It is no use*** = ***There is no use***，後面要接動名詞。
   > argue〔'ɑrgju〕*v.* 爭辯

6. (**C**) *There **being** no bus service*, I had to take a taxi.
因為沒有公車了，我只好坐計程車。

> 原句為 Because there was no bus service，省略連接詞
> Because，前後主詞不同須保留，was 改成 being。
> 本題常考，請注意。

7. (**B**) "Would you pass me the salt?" "<u>Here you are.</u>"
「請把鹽遞給我好嗎？」「拿去。」

> 將對方要的東西遞給對方時，可說 Here you are.。若東西為單數
> 名詞，也可說 Here it is.，複數則可用 Here they are.。

8. (**A**) Let's go to the movies *together*, **shall we**?
我們一起去看電影好嗎？

> Let's 開頭的句子表「提議」時，附加問句為 **shall we**。
> 在此 shall we = shall we go。Let's go 和 Let us go 句意不同。
> （詳見文法寶典 p.7）

9. (**A**) This vacuum cleaner is *highly* recommended *for **its** durability*.
這種真空吸塵器因其耐久性而被大力推薦。

> 主詞 vacuum cleaner 為物，代名詞所有格應用 **its**。it's 是 it is
> 的縮寫，不可與 its 混淆。
> vacuum (ˋvækjuəm) *n.* 真空   ***vacuum cleaner*** 真空吸塵器
> recommend (ˌrɛkəˋmɛnd) *v.* 推薦
> durability (ˌdjurəˋbɪlətɪ) *n.* 耐久

10. (**D**) Tom and Joe look alike. I *always **mistake*** one **for**
the other.
湯姆和喬看起來很像。我總是把一個誤認成另一個。

> ***mistake*** A **for** B 把 A 誤認成 B

TEST 48

Directions: *Of the four choices given after each sentence, choose the one most suitable for filling in the blank.*

1. "Do you think we'll have good weather?" "I hope _____."
   - (A) for
   - (B) it
   - (C) so
   - (D) to   ( )

2. There is no rule _____ has exceptions.
   - (A) but
   - (B) that
   - (C) without
   - (D) which   ( )

3. I'll have returned to America _____ this letter reaches you.
   - (A) if
   - (B) until
   - (C) by the time
   - (D) now that   ( )

4. He bought a new camera _____ two hundred dollars.
   - (A) by
   - (B) for
   - (C) in
   - (D) with   ( )

5. This machine did not function properly when it was delivered to my house. It _____ broken during shipping.
   - (A) can have
   - (B) could be
   - (C) has to be
   - (D) must have been   ( )

6. "Tomorrow our professor is going back to England."
   "I didn't know he _____."

   (A) had decided to leave
   (B) would have decided to leave
   (C) will decide to leave
   (D) is deciding to leave   (   )

7. Sarah demanded that she _____ given a refund.

   (A) is
   (B) be
   (C) will be
   (D) need be   (   )

8. My husband is an expert when it comes _____ Chinese food.

   (A) to cook
   (B) to cooking
   (C) of cooking
   (D) for cooking   (   )

9. The audience could not but _____ the performance of the pianist.

   (A) admire
   (B) to admire
   (C) admired
   (D) admiring   (   )

10. Will this much food _____ for a week's camping?

    (A) do
    (B) enough
    (C) all right
    (D) content   (   )

TEST 48 詳解

1.(**C**) "Do you think *we'll have good weather*?" "I hope ***so***."

「你認為天氣會好嗎?」「我希望如此。」

so 可當代名詞,代替名詞、名詞片語或子句,在此 so 代替 we'll
have good weather 一子句。

2.(**A**) There is ***no*** rule ***but*** *has exceptions*. 凡是規則必有例外。

but 為準關代,本身為否定意思,相當於 that…not,前面先行詞須有
否定字,以構成雙重否定。「no…without…」亦為雙重否定的用法,
但 without 是介系詞,不可接子句。

3.(**C**) I'll have returned to America ***by the time*** *this letter*

reaches you. 等到這封信寄到你手上時,我已經回到美國了。

by the time (*when*) = ***by the time*** (*that*) 表「到~時候」,
主要動詞通常用未來完成式。

4.(**B**) He ***bought*** a new camera ***for*** *two hundred dollars.*

他花了二百元美金買了一台新的相機。

表「買某物付多少錢」,要用「***buy sth. for*** (錢)」,或「***pay*** (錢)
for sth.」,介系詞 for 有表「交換」之意。

5.(**D**) This machine did not function *properly when it was delivered*

to my house. It ***must have been*** broken *during shipping.*

這台機器送到我家時已運作不佳。一定是在運送時弄壞了。

「***must have*** + *p.p.*」,表現在推測過去。

function (ˈfʌŋkʃən) *v.* 運作

deliver (dɪˈlɪvɚ) *v.* 遞送   shipping (ˈʃɪpɪŋ) *n.* 運送

6. (**A**) "*Tomorrow* our professor is going back to England."
"I **didn't** know he **had decided to leave**."

「明天我們教授就要回英國了。」「我不知道他已經決定要離開了。」

二個過去發生的動作，先發生者用過去完成式，後發生者用過去簡單式，在此，「決定離開」先發生，故用過去完成式。

7. (**B**) Sarah **demanded that** she **be** given a refund.

莎拉要求給予退錢。

demand〔dɪˈmænd〕*v.* 要求，為慾望動詞，接 that 子句，子句中助動詞要用 should，亦可省略。

refund〔ˈriˌfʌnd〕*n.* 退錢

8. (**B**) My husband is an expert *when it comes to cooking*

Chinese food. 一提到煮中國菜，我的丈夫是個專家。

when it comes to + V-ing 當一提到

9. (**A**) The audience **could not but** admire the performance

of the pianist. 觀眾禁不住讚歎這位鋼琴家的表演。

can / could not but + *V.* 禁不住；不得不（ = *can / could help* + *V-ing* = *can / could help but* + *V.*)（一定要看文法寶典 p.441）

audience〔ˈɔdɪəns〕*n.* 觀眾；聽眾　　admire〔ədˈmaɪr〕*v.* 讚賞

10. (**A**) Will this much food **do** *for a week's camping*?

這麼多的食物足夠露營一星期嗎？

本句缺乏動詞，故用 do，表「足夠；滿足需要」。

do = be good enough，在此為完全不及物動詞，

例如：That will do.（行行行。）

camping〔ˈkæmpɪŋ〕*n.* 露營

content〔kənˈtɛnt〕*adj.* 滿足的（形容人）

TEST 49

Directions: *Of the four choices given after each sentence, choose the one most suitable for filling in the blank.*

1. _____ students as Joe and Don need more encourage-
   ment from the teachers.
   - (A) So
   - (B) Such
   - (C) Like
   - (D) For example   ( )

2. In case of emergency, leave the building as quickly as
   possible _____.
   - (A) if instructed otherwise
   - (B) so instructed otherwise
   - (C) but otherwise instructed
   - (D) unless otherwise instructed   ( )

3. Her mother was busy _____ the dinner at that time.
   - (A) cooking
   - (B) to cook
   - (C) in cook
   - (D) for cooking   ( )

4. _____ are you moving the furniture for?
   - (A) What
   - (B) How
   - (C) Where
   - (D) Why   ( )

5. I may have to work, _____ I'll call you.
   - (A) for which
   - (B) in which case
   - (C) whereby
   - (D) wherefore   ( )

6. "Is Mary coming today?" "I _____. She is sick."
   - (A) don't suppose
   - (B) suppose her not
   - (C) suppose not
   - (D) don't suppose her to   (   )

7. The trouble is, _____ we get used to watching TV, we gradually come to watch it more and more.
   - (A) what
   - (B) so
   - (C) that
   - (D) once   (   )

8. It is high time that we _____ immediate action to solve the problem.
   - (A) took
   - (B) take
   - (C) must take
   - (D) to take   (   )

9. You can wear my scarf _____ you don't spill anything on it.
   - (A) as long as
   - (B) unless
   - (C) even if
   - (D) so that   (   )

10. It used to be difficult to enter university, but it is much easier than _____ now.
    - (A) any
    - (B) ever
    - (C) never
    - (D) once   (   )

TEST 49 詳解

1. (**B**) *Such* students *as Joe and Don* need more encouragement *from the teachers.* 像喬和唐這樣的學生需要老師們更多的鼓勵。

    such as「像是」可分開寫成 *such…as*，也可等於 like。(詳見文法寶典 p.125)

2. (**D**) *In case of emergency,* leave the building *as quickly as possible* *unless otherwise instructed.*

    萬一有緊急情況，除非有其他指示，否則儘快離開大樓。

    本句原為 … *unless you are otherwise instructed.* 由於句意明顯，而將 you are 省略。

    in case of 萬一發生   emergency〔ɪˈmɜdʒənsɪ〕*n.* 緊急情況
    otherwise〔ˈʌðə͵waɪz〕*adv.* 不同地；用別的方法
    instruct〔ɪnˈstrʌkt〕*v.* 指示

3. (**A**) Her mother *was busy cooking* the dinner *at that time.*
    她的媽媽當時正忙著煮晚餐。

    be busy (in) + V-ing 忙於做某事

4. (**A**) *What* are you moving the furniture *for*?
    你為什麼要移動傢俱呢？

    What…for 為什麼 (= *Why*)

5. (**B**) I may have to work, *in which case I'll call you.*
    我可能要上班，那樣的話，我會打電話給你。

    which 可做關係形容詞，修飾名詞 case，「關係形容詞＋名詞」，用法和關代一樣，引導形容詞子句。in this case「在這種情況下」；in that case「在那種情況下」；in which case 則指「在前面所說的那種情況下」。

6.(**C**) "Is Mary coming *today*?" "I suppose *not*. She is sick."

「瑪麗今天會來嗎？」「我想不會。她生病了。」

　　not 可代替否定子句，在此代替 that she is not coming today。

　　（一定要看文法寶典 p.129）

7.(**D**) The trouble is, *once* we get used to watching TV, we gradually come to watch it more and more.

問題是，我們一旦習慣看電視，就會慢慢越看越多。

　　once 爲連接詞，引導副詞子句 we get…TV，修飾後句動詞 come。

　　get used to + *N.* / *V-ing* 習慣於（= *get accustomed to*）

8.(**A**) It is high time that we *took* immediate action to solve the problem.

該是我們立刻採取行動來解決問題的時候了。

　　It is (*high*) *time* ｛ that S. + 過去式 / that S. + should + V. / for ~ to + V. ｝ 該是 ~ 做…的時候了

9.(**A**) You can wear my scarf *as long as* you don't spill anything on it. 只要你別把東西潑在我的圍巾上，你就可以戴。

　　連接詞 *as long as*「只要」，引導副詞子句，表條件；unless「除非」，even if「即使」，亦表條件，但句意不合；so that「如此」，爲因果關係用法，表結果，句意不合。

10.(**B**) It used to be difficult to enter university, but it is *much* easier *than ever* now.

過去進大學是很困難的，但現在比以前容易多了。

　　than ever 比以前

TEST 50

Directions: *Of the four choices given after each sentence, choose the one most suitable for filling in the blank.*

1. The pale look on his face suggested that he _____ afraid.
   - (A) is
   - (B) was
   - (C) be
   - (D) had been   ( )

2. What do you say _____ a cup of coffee?
   - (A) to have
   - (B) about having
   - (C) to having
   - (D) for having   ( )

3. We could do nothing _____ wait until the next morning.
   - (A) as
   - (B) but
   - (C) that
   - (D) with   ( )

4. It's a little cold. Would you mind _____ the window?
   - (A) me to close
   - (B) to close
   - (C) I close
   - (D) my closing   ( )

5. The heavy rain kept us _____ out yesterday.
   - (A) from going
   - (B) into going
   - (C) to go
   - (D) to be going   ( )

6. My father sat watching TV, _____ our dog, Babe, lying beside him.
   - (A) with
   - (B) by
   - (C) as
   - (D) to   (   )

7. We went to the restaurant he recommended, _____ was famous for its lamb chops.
   - (A) where
   - (B) which
   - (C) when
   - (D) how   (   )

8. It is such a heavy stone _____ he can't lift.
   - (A) whom
   - (B) that
   - (C) which
   - (D) as   (   )

9. _____ tourist naturally wants to see as much as possible of the country he is visiting.
   - (A) Any
   - (B) Some
   - (C) Few
   - (D) A lot of   (   )

10. Mr. Smith grew colder and colder _____ finally he got up and left the room.
    - (A) as
    - (B) than
    - (C) until
    - (D) whenever   (   )

TEST 50 詳解

1. (**B**) The pale look *on his face* suggested *that he __was__ afraid.*
   從他蒼白的臉色可看出，他很害怕。

   > suggest 在此表「暗示；透露出」，不是表「建議」，非慾望動詞用法，
   > 故用直說法。這題很重要，只有子句中表應該做某事的時候，才用 should。
   > （一定要看文法寶典 p.373 ）
   >
   > pale〔pel〕*adj.* 蒼白的

2. (**C**) ***What do you say __to__ having*** a cup of coffee?
   喝杯咖啡如何？

   > ***What do you say to*** + *V-ing* 做～如何（= *How about* + *V-ing*
   > = *What about* + *V-ing* ）

3. (**B**) We could ***do nothing __but__*** wait *until the next morning.*
   我們什麼也不能做，只能等到第二天早上。

   > ***do nothing but*** + *V.* 除了～之外什麼也不做；只是（= *only* ）

4. (**D**) It's *a little* cold. Would you ***mind __my closing__*** the window?
   有一點冷。你介意我把窗戶關上嗎？

   > mind 作「介意」解時，其後要接動名詞做受詞，動名詞意義上的主
   > 詞，若與主要子句的主詞不同，可用受格或所有格置於動名詞之前，
   > 故本題可用 my closing 或 me closing，也可接子句 if I close。

5. (**A**) The heavy rain ***kept*** us __*from*__ going out *yesterday.*
   昨天的大雨使我們無法外出。

   > $\begin{cases} \textbf{\textit{keep sb. from}} + \textbf{\textit{V-ing}} \ 阻止某人做某事 \\ = \textbf{\textit{stop sb. from}} + \textbf{\textit{V-ing}} \\ = \textbf{\textit{prevent sb. from}} + \textbf{\textit{V-ing}} \end{cases}$

6. (**A**) My father sat watching TV, **with** our dog, *Babe*, *lying beside him*. 爸爸坐著看電視，我們的狗，寶寶，躺在他旁邊。

「**with** ＋受詞＋分詞」表伴隨著主要動詞的情況。(詳見文法寶典 p.462)

7. (**B**) We went to the restaurant *he recommended*, **which** *was famous for its lamb chops.*
我們去了他推薦的那家餐廳，那裡的羊排很有名。

形容詞子句中，缺乏主詞，故關代應用 which，修飾先行詞 restaurant。
lamb (læm) *n.* 小羊　　chop (tʃɑp) *n.* 連骨的肉片
lamb chop 羊排

8. (**D**) It is **such** a heavy stone *as he can't lift.*
那是一塊他抬不起來的大石頭。

先行詞中有 such 時，關代要用 as，as 在形容詞子句中，做 lift 的
受詞，代替先行詞 stone。 (詳見文法寶典 p.159)

9. (**A**) ***Any*** tourist *naturally* wants to see as much as possible *of the country he is visiting.*
任何觀光客到了一個國家，當然都想儘可能多看一些風景。

any 可用於肯定句，指「任何一個」，some 可接單數或複數名詞，
但句意不合。
tourist ('turɪst) *n.* 觀光客

10. (**C**) Mr. Smith grew colder and colder **until** *finally he got up and left the room.*
史密斯先生覺得越來越冷，直到最後他終於起來，離開房間。

表示動作持續，直到某時，連接詞用 ***until***。

本書測驗題按照文法歸納

【2-⑥即指 Test 2 第 6 題】

1. 不定詞、動名詞、分詞

2-⑥，3-②、⑧，4-⑧，5-①，6-⑧、⑨，
7-④，8-⑤，9-⑧，10-①、③、⑨，
11-②，12-④，13-⑨、⑩，14-⑥、⑧，
15-②、⑨，16-②、③、④，17-②，
18-⑧、⑨，19-④、⑧、⑩，20-①，
22-④、⑤、⑦，23-①、⑥、⑧，24-⑤，
25-⑥、⑨，27-⑥，28-⑨，29-①，
30-⑦，31-⑧，32-①，33-①，33-⑤，
34-⑧，35-②，36-⑧，38-⑧，39-③、
⑥、⑨，40-①、⑤、⑩，41-⑤、⑨，
43-③，44-⑦，46-⑩，47-⑤、⑥，
48-⑨，49-③，50-③、④

2. 助動詞

1-⑥，2-⑩，8-①、④、⑥，10-②，
14-③、⑤，17-④、⑩，18-②，19-⑨，
21-⑤，27-④，28-⑩，31-⑨，33-⑦、⑩，
36-①，37-⑥，40-④，41-③，43-①，
44-⑤，45-⑨，48-⑤

3. 關係代名詞、關係副詞、 關係形容詞

3-⑨，5-⑤，8-③，9-③、④，11-①，
12-⑨，13-③，14-⑨，16-⑤、⑦，
21-⑧，23-⑤，25-②，26-⑦，28-③，
29-⑨，31-④、⑦，32-③，34-②，
35-⑥，36-⑩，39-⑧，40-④，41-②，
43-⑩，45-④，48-②，49-⑤，50-⑦、⑧

4. 假設法

1-①，3-①，4-⑨，11-⑧，13-⑥，
14-⑦，17-⑤，18-⑤，20-④、⑥，
23-⑩，24-④，27-⑤，30-⑥，31-⑩，
33-⑧，36-②，37-⑤，40-⑦，41-⑧，
45-⑩，49-⑧

5. 連接詞

2-②、③，4-⑦，6-①，7-⑥，9-②、⑥，
11-⑤、⑦，16-⑨，18-①、⑩，19-⑤，
21-②、③、⑨、⑩，22-②，26-⑧，
27-①，28-④，31-⑤，32-⑨、⑩，
34-③、⑤，35-④、⑤，38-⑥、⑦，
39-⑤，41-⑦，42-⑥，44-①，45-⑤，
46-⑤，48-③，49-②、⑦、⑨，50-⑩

6. 時態

4-①，11-⑨，15-⑦，20-⑨，27-③，
28-⑤，33-⑨，34-⑥，35-①、⑩，
37-③、④，38-⑨，40-②，41-⑥，
42-⑩，44-④，47-②，48-⑥

7. 形容詞

2-①、⑤，3-⑩，5-⑩，6-②、⑩，
10-⑩，13-⑦，16-⑥，17-①、③、⑦，
18-④，19-⑥，20-②，21-⑥，24-⑥，
25-⑤、⑩，26-②，27-⑧，29-④，
30-③，33-⑥，38-⑧，39-④，47-⑨，
50-⑨

8. 副詞

1-②、⑤、⑦、⑧、⑨，3-④、⑤、⑦，
4-④、⑥，6-⑦，7-①、⑤、⑦，9-⑦，
10-④、⑥、⑦，14-②，23-②，26-③，
27-⑨，29-⑤，30-④、⑩，32-④、⑦，
34-①，37-⑨、⑩，39-①，42-②，
43-⑥，46-⑨

9. 比較

1-④，6-④，7-②，8-⑦，9-①，10-⑧，
11-③、④，12-⑥，17-⑧，19-①、②，
24-⑧，26-④，27-⑩，29-⑥，31-①，
34-⑦、⑨，35-③，36-⑦，38-①，
40-⑧、⑨，42-③，43-④，45-①，
46-④，49-⑩

10. 動詞的用法

1-③，2-⑧，3-③，4-②，5-④、⑧，
6-⑤，7-⑧，8-⑧，9-⑩，10-⑤，
11-⑥，12-③、⑩，13-⑤，14-①，
15-⑥、⑧，16-⑩，17-⑥、⑨，18-⑦，
19-③、⑦，21-⑦，22-⑦、⑨、⑩，
23-④，24-③、⑦、⑨、⑩，26-①，
27-⑦，28-⑧，29-②、③，30-③、⑤、⑧，
31-②，33-②、③、④，34-④，35-⑨，
36-③、④，37-⑦、⑧，38-③，39-②，
40-⑥，43-⑦、⑧，44-⑥、⑧，45-⑧，
46-③，47-③，48-⑦、⑩，50-①、⑤

11. 名詞的用法

2-⑨，4-⑤、⑩，12-⑦，13-⑧，
16-①、⑧，20-⑧，23-③，25-①，
26-⑥，28-①，29-⑦，31-②，32-⑥，
34-⑩，39-⑩，41-④，42-④、⑨，
43-⑤

12. 代名詞的用法

1-⑩，5-⑥、⑦、⑨，6-⑥，9-⑤，
12-①、②、⑧，15-⑩，20-⑤、⑦、⑩，
21-①，22-⑥，23-⑦，24-②，25-⑦，
26-⑤，28-②，29-⑧，31-③，32-⑤，
38-②、⑩，39-⑦，41-①，42-⑤、⑦，
43-⑨，45-②、③、⑦，46-⑦，48-①，
49-①、⑥

13. 介系詞的用法

2-④，5-②、③，7-③、⑩，8-⑩，11-⑩，
14-④，20-③，21-④，22-①，24-①，
25-④、⑧，26-⑨，29-⑩，30-①，
31-⑥，32-③，35-⑦，36-⑤、⑨，
37-①、②，41-⑩，42-①、⑧，43-②，
44-⑩，45-⑥，46-①、⑧，47-①、
④、⑩，48-④、⑧，50-②、⑥

14. 省略

8-②，12-⑤，13-①，27-②

15. 主詞與動詞的一致

7-⑨，13-②，14-⑩，25-③，26-⑩，
28-⑥，30-②，44-②、③，46-②

16. 疑問詞

4-③，15-①，22-③，23-⑨，28-⑦，
38-⑤，47-⑧，49-④

17. 排列

3-⑥，9-⑨，15-⑤，18-⑥，36-⑥，
44-⑨，46-⑥，47-⑦

18. 否定

6-③，8-⑨，13-④，15-③

·心得筆記欄·

•心得筆記欄•

劉毅英文家教班成績優異同學獎學金排行榜

姓 名	學 校	總金額	姓 名	學 校	總金額	姓 名	學 校	總金額
潘羽薇	丹鳳高中	21100	高士權	建國中學	7600	賴奕均	松山高中	3900
孔爲亮	中崙高中	20000	吳鴻鑫	中正高中	7333	戴寧昕	師大附中	3500
吳文心	北一女中	17666	謝宜廷	樹林高中	7000	江紫寧	大同高中	3500
賴柏盛	建國中學	17366	翁子惇	縣格致中學	6900	游清心	師大附中	3500
劉記齊	建國中學	16866	朱浩廷	陽明高中	6500	陳蓁	海山高中	3500
張庭碩	建國中學	16766	張毓	成淵高中	6500	曾清翎	板橋高中	3400
陳瑾慧	北一女中	16700	吳宇珊	景美女中	6200	吳昕儒	中正高中	3400
羅培恩	建國中學	16666	王昱翔	延平高中	6200	高正岳	方濟高中	3250
毛威凱	建國中學	16666	張祐誠	林口高中	6100	林夏竹	新北高中	3100
王辰方	北一女中	16666	游霈晴	靜修女中	6000	曾昭惠	永平高中	3000
李俊逸	建國中學	16666	林彥君	大同高中	6000	萬彰允	二信高中	3000
溫彥瑜	建國中學	16666	張騰升	松山高中	6000	張晨	麗山國中	3000
葉乃元	建國中學	16666	陳姿穎	縣格致中學	5900	廖泓恩	松山工農	3000
邱御碩	建國中學	16666	沈怡	復興高中	5800	張意涵	中正高中	2900
劉橿坤	松山高中	14400	莊永瑋	中壢高中	5600	劉冠伶	格致高中	2900
張凱俐	中山女中	13333	邱鈺璘	成功高中	5600	鄭翔文	格致高中	2800
邱馨荷	北一女中	12000	許斯閎	丹鳳高中	5500	莊益昕	建國中學	2700
陳瑾瑜	北一女中	11700	郭子豪	師大附中	5400	葉禹岑	成功高中	2700
施哲凱	松山高中	10450	黃韻蓉	東吳大學	5400	李承絃	復興高中	2600
陳宇翔	成功高中	10333	陸冠宏	師大附中	5200	林郁婷	北一女中	2600
林上軒	政大附中	10000	李柏霆	明倫高中	5100	張淨雅	北一女中	2600
陳玟妤	中山女中	9000	孫廷瑋	成功高中	5100	許茵茵	東山高中	2600
林泇欣	格致高中	8800	李泓霖	松山高中	5000	范容菲	慧燈高中	2500
黃敏頤	大同高中	8600	劉若白	大同高中	5000	孔爲鳴	高 中 生	2500
蘇玉如	北一女中	8400	洪菀妤	師大附中	5000	廖永皓	大同高中	2500
廖奕翔	松山高中	8333	洪宇謙	成功高中	5000	蘇翊文	格致高中	2300
廖克軒	成功高中	8333	黃柏誠	師大附中	5000	陳歆	景文高中	2300
呂承翰	師大附中	8333	劉其瑄	中山女中	5000	邱國正	松山高中	2300
鮑其鈺	師大附中	8333	陳韋廷	成功高中	5000	許晉嘉	成功高中	2200
簡珞帆	高 中 生	8333	李維任	成功高中	5000	林靜宜	蘭陽女中	2200
蕭羽涵	松山高中	8333	林晉陽	師大附中	4900	吳玟慧	格致高中	2200
廖奕翔	松山高中	8333	林品君	北一女中	4900	吳珮彤	再興高中	2100
蕭若浩	師大附中	8333	柯季欣	華江高中	4500	張榕	南港高中	2000
連偉宏	師大附中	8333	李智傑	松山高中	4300	張媛瑄	景美女中	2000
王舒亭	縣格致中學	8300	許博勳	松山高中	4300	胡明媛	復興高中	2000
楊政勳	中和高中	8100	張鈞堯	新北高中	4166	盧世軒	徐匯中學國中部	2000
鄭鈺立	建國中學	8000	林子薰	中山女中	4000	陳新雅	新北高中	2000
吳宇晏	南港高中	8000	王思予	林口高中	4000	黃子晏	私立大同高中	2000
楊沐焓	師大附中	7750	鄭字彤	樹林高中	4000	蔡雅淳	秀峰高中	2000
謝育姍	景美女中	7600	張心瑜	格致高中	3900			

劉毅英文教育機構

台北本部：台北市許昌街17號6F（捷運M8出口對面·學習補習班）
台中總部：台中市三民路三段125號7F（光南文具批發樓上·劉毅補習班）
www.learnschool.com.tw

TEL：（02）2389-5212
TEL：（04）2221-8861

本書製作過程

　　本書每一條題目，均摘自國內外大學入學試題，Test 1 至 Test 25，由謝靜芳老師負責，Test 26 至 Test 50，由蔡琇瑩老師負責，每題均經劉毅老師及美籍老師 Laura E. Stewart，和 Andy Swarzman 詳細校訂，本資料經劉毅英文家教班 3000 多位同學使用後，效果十分顯著，大家對文法都變得有信心，喜歡做文法題目。

> 　　看了解說還不懂，怎麼辦？可直接打電話給劉毅老師。
>
> **劉毅老師文法解答專線：(02) 2239-5480**

中級英語文法測驗

主　　　編 / 劉　毅

發　行　所 / 學習出版有限公司　　　☎ (02) 2704-5525

郵 撥 帳 號 / 05127272 學習出版社帳戶

登　記　證 / 局版台業 2179 號

印　刷　所 / 裕強彩色印刷有限公司

台 北 門 市 / 台北市許昌街 10 號 2 F　　☎ (02) 2331-4060

台灣總經銷 / 紅螞蟻圖書有限公司　　　☎ (02) 2795-3656

本公司網址　www.learnbook.com.tw

電 子 郵 件　learnbook@learnbook.com.tw

售價：新台幣一百八十元正

2016 年 9 月 1 日新修訂

ISBN 957-519-554-X